Who Owns Us?

A Novel

Loretta J. Krause

Note: Louis T. McFadden was a Pennsylvania Congressman from the Fifteenth District (1915-1935) who opposed the Federal Reserve. His obituary shows he had a son. Other aspects of this genealogy are fiction, as are names, characters, places, and situations within the novel. They take life from the author's creativity and are intended as fiction only.

DEDICATION

This book is dedicated to my family. May they grow up in a world that values humanity more than mammon, and freedom of thought and expression

1

'X' MARKS THE ROCK

He was a burly man, ruddy face, about six feet two with massive shoulders and arms. He had been fracking more than two decades, some in West Texas, now in Pennsylvania, and he knew everything about drilling a fracker needed to know. He should have been commander by now, but he wasn't. That simple. "BE," his company logo, was impressed into the left side of his dark green uniform. Yellow hardhat tilted to its side; Gary approached his supervisor.

About ten years older and an inch or so taller than his foreman, Frank Goring glanced up from his schematics then looked at his watch. "What is it, Gary? I gave the order to start clearing the field a half hour ago."

"We started when you said; the excavators are ready to go, but there's something odd about one of the rocks out there," the foreman said. "Like a message of some kind.

We could ignore it, break it apart or roll it away, but maybe you'd want to see it first."

Frank gesticulated with a shrug. "A rock is a rock; color, shape or size doesn't matter. What's odd about it?"

There's an X on it, a big X, and there's a name under it - or maybe it's a place. Dan noticed it when he stomped down on the overgrowth around it. We cleared it away. It's not dirt; it's a mark all right, and a word that could be a name.

A rock with an X and what might be a name? Frank threw down his clip board and motioned Gary to lead.

First day on the job and a complication already. Constructing this pad would take long as it was. If the terrain had been flat, it might have taken little more than week, but this terrain was hilly and rocky. Laying the pad for this site might take a month before trucks, drills and other equipment could come in; so Frank did not need a delay. But since he was meticulous in every aspect of his job, he'd see what Gary was talking about. They had worked together fifteen years, long enough for him to appreciate Gary's instincts. No reason to ignore them now.

They walked the length of the field that would become a 350 square foot construction pad, the base for trucks filled with sand, water and lubricant needed to frack the Marcellus shale here in Bradford County.

Because this site was the most difficult, Frank had decided to lay the first pad here, start the drilling, then move to sites with flatter terrain that BE had licenses to drill. If he didn't meet the deadline on each lease, he'd lose it. Maybe the owner would ask for more money or go with another company that was offering more. Property owners were asking more for the use of their land and prices were going up fast.

Meeting his timeline was important. Get this one started then begin another. Eventually he'd put six or more wells on this site, the same number on the other sites. Hopefully, they would bring up enough natural gas to make their company top producer for the year, maybe the next decade. But he had to start them first.

Half the distance away, he saw the men milling beside a brown smooth-shaped rock butting up from a relatively flat surface. It was big, but they had seen bigger. Any excavator could pick it up in its mammoth jaws and relocate it like a twig. As he got close enough to see nuances, he saw the X painted near the rock's base on the side facing him. Closer, and he saw the word, maybe a name of some kind, directly under it.

"So what name, or whose?" Frank said, examining it closely, brushing off remnants of soil, moss, and mold that had worn into some letters and distorted others. It was legible. "Mc . . . McFa . . . . Anyone hear the name 'McFadden'?"

Gary and five others shrugged. The name meant nothing to them, but the sixth stared and scratched his chin. "My daddy mentioned that name a few times when I was a kid. My family's local. I grew up here and my daddy before me. Not a whole lot he didn't know about the place or its history, and he said that name several times. Think it goes back a ways."

"Remember anything he said?" Frank asked.

Dan, weather worn from sun that made him look older than his age, shook his head. "Not a whole lot. Daddy didn't say a whole lot about anything, and I was a kid, maybe four, five. I only remember it because it was right after Kennedy was killed. That I remember. Daddy was cursing, and putting Kennedy and whatever it was, together with McFadden, a congressman from around here decades ago. He stopped cursing when my momma got scared. Then he shut up. Never said another word about it. A five year old kid doesn't get caught up with a dead president or a dead congressman. A bat and a ball, that's all." Dan smiled, thinking about youth. "But yeah, I remember the name."

"Okay," Frank said, "dig a couple feet; see if we find something. If not, we move the rock and lay the pad."

A few whacks with the excavator plus human muscle devoted to hand shoveling, and the men were banging into a heavy metal "thunk." From the dark earth, they struggled to bring up a strongbox. "Well, I'll be damned," Dan commented. "It's there."

"What's there?" Gary asked.

"Nothin, just a rumor about buried treasure teenagers like to repeat."

The box, about two feet by one and a half, took some effort to exhume even with three strong men taking turns shoveling a bigger hole to pull it out. It was wedged tightly into a crevice, and when they finally got it up, it was caked in black soil that clung to its steel as though a symbiosis had been born in that dark crypt. Gary brushed the top clean and read the inscription, "WPH." A strong lock secured its contents from scrutiny.

"Looks like your instincts were right, Gary," Frank said, "but WPH has nothing to do with 'McFadden.'"

"Wanna bust it open?"

Frank shook his head. "Think I'll take it to the van and wait for the property owner to get it."

"That might be weeks, Frank," Dan commented, "or never."

"No, he's here, staying a few miles down the road. He's coming today - wants to oversee the job."

The men groaned. Another property owner breathing down their necks, scrutinizing every shovel, every bit, every step of the process.

"Claims he won't interfere," Frank said, reading their minds.

The men mumbled and griped in disbelief as Frank hoisted the strongbox to his shoulder and headed to the van. Didn't matter; they had a job to do no matter what property owner was coming.

2

A SPITFIRE REPORTER

Wade Henderson crossed the field about 8:45. Morning was crisp, typical for a mid-March day. Growing up here as a young boy, he had always loved the vastness of the fields, the smell of earth being tilled, crops growing and tall grasses flowing. He had spent many days exploring wooded areas, startling small woodland creatures who scuttled into hiding once discovered. But that was more than twenty-five years ago.

All that remained of those memories was a summer house his mom had bought and converted to a bed and breakfast twenty years ago so she could remove herself from city life, crowds, concrete, busses and carbon dioxide emissions when that toxic lifestyle became too oppressive. The inn was still operational, but not by her.

The place was run by a professional staff now, a staff that always welcomed Wade. Even if the inn were full, Peggy, the manager, would find a room for him. When he had called, she was ecstatic. "Of course, Mr. Wade, anytime. We're booked full, so we'll be crowded, but there's a room for you." That warmth could draw Wade back anytime, and he welcomed it at this time in his life more than ever.

The land had been in his family for a few generations, generations he had never known, but aside from the acreage his dad had sold long ago, it had been family-owned for close to one hundred years. That meant he wasn't going to sully the family name by letting this fracking process, new to this county, hurt the community. Even if he didn't know his roots, they were important. His mother had instilled that in him.

Wade approached the first worker he saw. "Frank Goring?" The man nodded and pointed towards a long, silver van, bigger than a large mobile home, the kind in which more than a few residents of this area lived. Fortunately for the drillers, they would be living in hotels or motels in town. Then there was also the 'man camp' Best Energy had erected that would hold more than two hundred fifty men. Between this well-site and the others, they would be working round the clock, fifty men per shift, every day for a long time.

The door was open, inviting Wade to walk in as he knocked. Two men, both in dark green uniforms, turned. One stood at least three inches over six feet, muscular, fair complexion with a full head of white hair that belied his age. The second man was about the same height, bulkier around the middle but younger. Both men had been examining something rectangular and solid, a box, metal of some kind, secured with a heavier than necessary lock for a box that size. Clumps of dirt adhered to it; some littered the floor.

"Morning gentlemen," Wade said politely. He was taller than both men. "I'm Wade Henderson. I own this property."

"Mr. Henderson," Frank nodded and turned towards Wade with an outstretched hand. "Glad to meet you. I know who you are from the licenses. I'm Frank Goring and this is my right-hand man, Gary Wallace."

Gary extended his hand. Introductions over, Frank directed Wade's attention to the box. We found this a short while ago buried under a large rock which had an X on it and the name "McFadden" under it. It's your land; so it's your box, but we're curious. Know anyone by that name?"

The name was familiar only because street signs in this county bore that name when he was young, not because of familial ties. They were just sign posts with a name, like Little Creek or Jones Cove, leading to a fishing hole, what he cared about then.

"Can't say I do, but I'd be interested in knowing what's in it, 'specially since it's mine."

"Okay then," Frank said.

He nodded to Gary who reached for a heavy crow bar and sledge hammer. "Think we'll need these. This lock's not gonna give up easily."

And it didn't. Lots of whacks later, the hinge sprung. They stepped back to let Wade open it. Wade, in work gear and boots, wasn't concerned about getting dirt on his hands or clothes, but he was surprised it took so much strength to pop the top. They needed a metal wedge and hammer to open its seam.

Wade lifted the top slowly. Nothing alive in here, that was certain. But who knows what he'd find. Slowly, with resistance and lots of screeches from rusty hinges, the lid finally opened. The men stared at orderly piles of neatly wrapped bills, two-dollar bills to be exact. Wade pulled up a pack and examined it. "A stack of two's, neatly wrapped, with another layer underneath, maybe a third? Doesn't make much sense. Two-dollar bills?" He wacked the packet against his palm, thinking. "Don't know when these were buried, say thirty-five, forty years ago or more. Maybe there's fifty in each pack. Probably several thousand dollars in here, but that wasn't a fortune, not even then. So why all the fuss and secrecy? Hardly worth it, when the person could have deposited these bills in a bank, or spent them."

"They could buy a lot more then," Gary said.

"But they couldn't make someone wealthy. This isn't some family fortune, even if it were a poor family. It has purchasing power, but not enough to devise a plan and take the time and energy to store it in a metal box, dig a deep hole and hide it underground. This person did not want these bills in a bank."

At that moment, another tap at the door was followed by the prettiest face Wade had ever seen. Frank and Gary must have agreed because it stopped the three of them in mid-speech. She was a complete stranger, so what was she doing here, at a fracking site in the making?

"Good morning, gentlemen. I'm Stevie Komsky, the press." She motioned to the credentials around her neck. "I called yesterday to say I was coming for a story about hydraulic fracturing, or fracking, as it's commonly termed. I spoke to a man named Frank."

Frank regained whatever composure he had lost and returned to business mode. "That's me. Yes, I remember. You're doing a story on fracking coming into Bradford

County. But I told you that you won't see the drilling process until we lay the pad, which starts today but will take about a month."

"Yes, you did say that, but I convinced my editor to let me drive up for an early start. I want to see the land before anything is done to it, take a few pictures, sort of a before and after feature. I'm also hoping to interview some of the locals and property owners and get their input. You know, why they're selling drilling rights for fracking; what they think it will do to their economy and the environment, things like that. If I get what I need this weekend, I'll come back in a month. The trucks should be working by then."

She smiled. Frank had to force himself not to, despite her riveting gaze and piercing blue eyes. His work and demeanor were always professional. Then Stevie noticed the strongbox with dirt pooled around it and clumps covering the floor. "What's this?" She asked, moving closer. "Looks like buried treasure."

"Just some two-dollar bills some eccentric buried on my property," Wade replied.

"Your property? You own this land? Perfect. I could start my interviews with you. And we could investigate this money you found on your land."

"Wait, Ma'am," Wade said. "This is not a partnership. There's no 'we' investigating anything."

"Aren't you curious as to how or why this box got buried on your land and so long ago?" She got close to the box, flicked away a few clumps of dirt and looked inside. "Mind if I take a peek?"

"Why not," Wade heard the sarcasm in his voice, "you've just about put your head in it already."

10

The men stepped aside as Stevie inched her way between them. Frank looked at his watch. "It's 9:10, Gary. Let's get started." They made a hasty exit, leaving Wade and the reporter to spar on their own. "That's danger," Frank commented more to himself than to Gary.

"What is?" Gary replied anyway.

"Her. That reporter. Did you see the way she was dressed?"

Gary walked in step with his foreman, not saying a word. The reporter wore casual jeans, work boots, a cable knit sweater over a long-sleeved collar shirt. What was Frank thinking?

3

NO 'WE' IN RESEARCH

Inside the control van, Stevie picked up a packet of bills and shuffled through it, examining the front and back. "You sure it's nothing?" She asked.

Wade looked at her quizzically.

"When was it issued?"

"How would I know? I saw it for the first time before you walked in. Haven't had time to trace serial numbers."

Not a pleasant man to approach, Stevie thought. "Well, they're not greenbacks," she murmured more to herself than to Wade, "but if this were issued in the early 60's, there could be some historical significance."

"Explain . . . please." The "please," was an afterthought, an attempt to ameliorate his harsh tone.

"I'm not sure, but . . ." she pulled up several more packs, flipped them over and curled back the wrapping. "They say The United States of America, not Federal Reserve Note, and two-dollar bills? I've never even seen one . . . and what's this?"

A corner of plain, no-longer-white paper had eked through the tightly packed wads when she pulled up the middle pack. As she pulled it up, she exposed a folded paper. Stevie put the money in the box, pulled out the paper, unfolded it and read. "Who owns us? Research McFadden, JFK, et al."

She looked at Wade. "What does this mean? We know JFK, but who's McFadden?"

Wade shrugged. "Seems the owner of this strongbox was obsessed with some guy McFadden whose name is on a few street signs in this area. 'McFadden' was also written on the rock where this box was buried."

"Some guy wrote this name on a rock? Woah, this *is* becoming a mystery." Her face lit up. "You know nothing about him? Maybe he lived around here. We could search Records or the Historic Society," she said and looked at Wade with a mischievous glint that broadened her smile, making her prettier than she already was."

"I said there's no 'we.' You want to research this guy, go ahead, but you'll have to do it on your own. If he lived here, it had to be a very long time ago. My parents were born here, and I don't recall them ever mentioning that name."

"Maybe they did but you never noticed."

"Look, go back to New York, or wherever you came from; come back in a month, get your story and be done. There's nothing to keep you in this town, or me either." Wade threw the bills in the box and slammed it shut, ready to hoist it and leave.

"WPH?" Stevie saw the initials on the lid and turned to Wade. "Do you know anything about WPH?"

13

"Never heard of him, or her." He leaned into the box, grabbed its handles, and walked off with it hanging at his side.

4

POLLY'S B&B

---

olly's Bed and Breakfast served a delicious breakfast. Melon and cantaloupe balls filled a crystal bowl. Strawberries and blueberries topped with powdered sugar filled another. Bacon, country ham, scrambled eggs, and hash browns filled serving platters that covered the long buffet table. Hot biscuits came straight from the oven; coffee dripped, hot water decanters poured for tea; cream, sugar, at their side. Trays of croissants, sweet rolls, and tarts, all home-baked, made Stevie go back for seconds.

She sat at a table-for-two in the far corner of this country cottage with white embroidered tablecloths, napkins and matching valences that gave the windows a lacy look. And rather than earthenware plates and cups, all the dishware was fine china, powder blue borders and gold trimmed rims. Very delicate.

This was delightful. Stevie was enjoying her second cup of coffee, sipping slowly, inhaling its aroma and not in a hurry to leave, when a male voice intruded on her thoughts.

"I wouldn't ask, but yours is the only table with an available seat."

Stevie nodded and Wade, his plate filled with eggs, bacon and just about everything else, seated himself comfortably opposite her.

"I had no idea you were staying at this inn too. Aren't there hotels or motels where fracking crews stay?"

"There are, but I stay here because I know the owner, and, as you can see, they have the best breakfast in Bradford County, maybe in the entire state. Whenever I need a break from city-life, I come here. Now, I'm out here because of the drilling. Want to make sure everything goes smoothly, since it's my property." Then his eyes met hers with intensity. "And no, I don't stay with the workers. Why would I?"

Of course he wouldn't. He was right, why would he? An obvious prejudice on her part. "I shouldn't have said that. I apologize. I thought, in error, that a one month stay would be expensive, at least for me it would." Her smile was genuine.

Wade nodded his acceptance. "I misunderstood. But no, I am not staying with the workers, and no I am not staying the month, just one or two days on a weekend. I do work, and I have to get back."

"To where, if that's not a personal question."

"Same as you – New York."

"I live," she paused, not wanting to be too specific, "on the other side of the Hudson." He nodded, not asking where. She was glad for that. "But on another point, you were candid about this being your property; so why were you so secretive about the McFadden name?"

He put his fork down. "Secretive?" He shook his head. "What are you talking about?"

"'McFadden', the name on the rock and in the strongbox. You said you had never heard the name, except maybe on a street sign. But I went to both the Records Department and the Historic Society yesterday and the McFadden name is there, definitely there. Yet you pretended to know nothing about it. Why?"

"Pretended? Why? Isn't that like being assumed guilty before trial, or is this some kind of reporter's technique to intimidate an answer? Because if it is, I don't appreciate it at all."

His response surprised her. She had assumed he had known who McFadden was but hadn't wanted to reveal it. Maybe he didn't know. It was possible.

"You're right. I did assume you knew, and that you had avoided it because it was none of my business, and it isn't. But when I went to Records and Archives at the Historic Society, the name appeared prominently in the early 1900's, and . . . ." She paused, wondering if he would welcome or reject the truth.

"And what? Go ahead, Miss Komsky, finish your sentence."

"And from what I found . . . you are related to McFadden. To be exact, he is your great grandfather."

Wade froze, speechless. Some guy he had never heard of except for his name on a street sign was his great grandfather?

Stevie was taken aback. Maybe he really didn't know. "Mr. Henderson," she stated formally, "have you ever been to either place?"

He glared. "To Records, or the Historic Society? Are you serious? I was eight when my parents moved to New York. Were you ever in the Department of Records or the Historic Society in your town at eight, Miss Komsky? Were you ever there at all?"

He had her there. If no one in his family had ever mentioned McFadden, how would he know? Generations have a way of losing themselves in the past. In her own lifetime, she only knew her father, who was killed when the Marine Barracks in Lebanon were bombed in '83, and whatever her mother had told her about her grandmother, who died years before she was born.

"It seems I owe you another apology, Mr. Henderson." She felt herself flush. "I should leave." She put her cup down, collected her purse and sweater. "Enjoy your breakfast, Mr. Henderson. But for the record, McFadden had a son and a daughter, and his daughter married a Henderson, William Patrick Henderson." She emphasized first, middle, and last names, WPH.

Her exit was quick. She had packed the night before, and was glad she had. She was out of Polly's in fifteen minutes. A month would pass before she would have to come back. Maybe Wade Henderson would not be here when she did.

5

BIG MONEY'S FOES

The drive home was invigorating. A hint of spring was in the air; "Elusive Butterfly" was playing on an oldies station, birds chirped loudly enough to be heard through her window, and an occasional hawk floated above looking for its morning meal. Four hours wasn't a long trip, and, along with continuous 80's music, she had uninterrupted time to reflect on her encounter with Mr. Wade Henderson and what she had learned from her research yesterday.

Louis T. McFadden had represented Pennsylvania's Fifteenth District for twenty years. The outspoken foe of international bankers, he had chaired the House Banking and Currency Committee for twelve years. He knew his stuff. "Bet he made a ton of enemies going after the Federal Reserve," Stevie said out loud, interrupting A-ha's 'Take on Me,' "enough to get him killed."

Big money didn't like opposition, that she realized when she had done a paper about Lincoln while she was in college. He had opposed the New York Bankers when they offered to lend him money to finance the Civil War with interest rates as high as 25%. Pricey, so, Lincoln printed his own money independent of the bankers and owed them no interest. A hint towards his assassination? That was the 1860's; McFadden was the 1930's, and JFK's in the 1960's.

Was it a coincidence that they had gone against banking interests and all had been assassinated, with three attempts on McFadden's life. Anyone else? Hmm, that was a challenging and multi-faceted question, but filling in those time periods might provide evidence and connect an assassination with Wade's strongbox. She shook her head. This was way beyond them, or beyond her, anyway. Wade wanted no part of any investigation.

But the money could be for something more personal, like finding the missing part of a family. Someone had gone through a lot of trouble to keep those bills out of a bank and include a note. Who owns us might lead to clues and a family reuniting. She'd research Wade's family tree again when she had time.

But she didn't have time. She had a job, and a hectic one. She had to concentrate on the stories she did have to write, the big one looming ahead from an aloof fracking commander, and those due this week. Besides, it was not difficult to realize if big banks had co-opted our Constitution to create the Federal Reserve, what could Stevie Komsky, a nobody, be able to find? Nothing.

She turned left from the Marginal Highway and headed up Kingswood Ave to the Bluff, thinking of stories she'd be submitting this week. Her article about the Ides of March was due tomorrow, running Wednesday. She had finished it before the weekend. She'd add one special touch before submitting it for print, the soothsayer in *Julius Caesar.*

Her second story would run Friday, a human interest article on the St. Patrick's Day parade. This needed a bit more. She would cover the first St. Patty's parade in New York City, 1762, and how the parades grew. She'd include a few quotes from the mayor, fire chief and other officials whom she had already interviewed, and she'd go one step further – she'd weave a little history in it about St. Patrick, who had been kidnapped at sixteen from his home in Britain and taken to Ireland as a slave. Escaping six years later, he studied in the Catholic Church for the next fifteen years and returned, of all places, to Ireland as a missionary. Thirty years later, because of his work, Ireland was almost entirely Christian. She wanted some of that in her article along with parades and quotes from politicians.

Stevie had more than enough to do; she couldn't concern herself with a congressman who had died seventy years ago. No matter how inquisitive she was, she had gone to PA for a story about fracking. Focus on that; forget the rest.

But the one feeling she couldn't shake was that her assumptions about Wade had been wrong. She had dropped the McFadden information on him thinking he had known. From his reaction, she realized he had no idea McFadden was his great grandfather. That must have hurt. Couple that with his grandfather's initials on the strongbox, and she was surprised he hadn't gotten up and walked out before her. She should have been more tactful.

Maybe she could make amends. She had a month before she had to return to Bradford County for her story, but she could go back in a week to talk to him, if he'd let her, if he'd be there. He said he was going up on a regular basis; maybe their visits could coincide. She'd do it. She'd book her arrival for Friday and see if Peggy would talk about Wade's next visit. It had possibilities, and by then she would be able to think of some peace offering.

6

STEVIE'S ULTIMATE STORY

The week disappeared like an "abracadabra," but then most weeks seemed to be evaporating like that since she graduated from Princeton seven years ago with an M.A. in English and a minor in journalism.

Getting a job as a cub reporter for the *Tribune* directly after graduation, she had written some outstanding copy on political issues affecting the state and Central Jersey, and a few about education that caught some flack when she addressed state testing, but the piece that was picked up by the Associated Press and snagged by the *Times* was her 9-11 article.

September 11, 2001, a day no person living at that time would ever forget, another "Day that would live in Infamy." Other reporters had headed to Ground Zero for eyewitness coverage, but Stevie, instead of interviewing first responders for what they had lived through, dressed in firefighter gear and took herself down as far as the press was allowed to get the real feel.

Then the unexpected happened: she was mistaken for a first responder. Blundering her way through pulverized cement and smoldering debris, she was caught up in a rescue effort to dig out a crypt where three people, barely alive, had been trapped over eight hours. Forgetting the legal consequences, she poured her heart into the rescue mission and worked with every bit of strength to free the victims.

Their efforts were rewarded when two women and a young child were pulled out from that tomb, transferred to gurneys and whisked away to St. Vincent's Hospital, but not before Stevie had removed her mask, and her press credentials were in full view. The younger woman, semi-conscious, had looked up at her. Amid tears, her voice hoarse and weak, she whispered, "Tell my husband I love him."

Stevie stood mesmerized. She imagined Samir, dead, lying on the hard ground, with his wife Rachel, at his side. She stood transfixed, not caring about the onslaught from fire officials and police when they realized she was the press. What saved her was a borough president's praise for her heroic efforts. Suddenly and unwittingly, she was elevated to heroic status, and her story secured her a job at the *Times*.

That's when her mom and stepfather set her up in an apartment on Bergenline Ave in Weehawken, NJ, overlooking New York's skyline. The apartment would be temporary, but so close to the City it was perfect. Hop on a bus or a shuttle, and you're there.

"See if you like it," her mom had said. "If you and the job fit, we'll get you something permanent, a house if you prefer, big enough so we can stay over, see a play, go to the Met, do things people do in New York. And no, we won't interfere in your life."

Two years later, her apartment on Bergenline morphed into a house on Kings Bluff, for her, outrageously expensive, but her stepfather insisted. He gutted the kitchen, made a few additional upgrades, and sent his staff from his mansion in Princeton to Weehawken with Thomas, his limo driver. They cleaned every room in the house, every nook, from baseboard to the ceiling until it sparkled while Sarah, his culinary manager for decades, cooked and froze enough for two week's worth of dinners. She refused to let her adopted daughter, as she called Stevie, go hungry or eat fast, garbage food. It was a "pinch me" experience. Stevie and her mother, who had experienced so much tragedy, were completely happy.

As she turned onto route 6, she reminisced about the past and how quickly it leaves us behind. She also considered the present, why she was here, and if Wade would arrive tomorrow as Peggy had indicated, to check the fracking progress. According to Peggy, he would be there by late afternoon, which was good. Stevie would have time to settle in and visit the fracking site in the morning; talk to Frank Goring without interruption. Maybe he'd be more amenable and smile. Maybe she'd get to talk to more locals too.

7

BECAUSE OF THE FED?

Noon on Friday morphed past 4:00 p.m. when Stevie pulled into Polly's rustic-looking lodge. The lot was quite full. Stevie wondered what attracted so many people to this part of PA on a weekend. What's to do here? Nothing much, and maybe that was the draw.

She hoisted one large, swivel-wheeled suitcase from the trunk of her Buick Rendezvous, new in 2002, and just fine four years later. She loved this car. Plenty big enough and over twenty-five miles per gallon highway driving, V6, silver gray, it was perfect for her needs.

Peggy greeted her at the door. Such warmth, Stevie almost didn't trust it, but a hug coupled with a wide smile could disarm just about anybody. "Dinner starts at 5:30 and you don't want to be late." She put her hand to her mouth as if to whisper. "Prime rib, mashed potatoes, green beans and cornbread, home baked of course."

She couldn't miss that. She hurried through the foyer, decorated in St Patrick's Day green, leprechaun figurines adorning the fireplace mantle with green streamers hung from the ceiling corners, cascading into a full bouquet of green carnations hanging from the center chandelier.

Once in her room, same room as last week, she plopped on the bed to unwind for a half hour and almost fell asleep. Then she set about unpacking and freshening up; changing from jeans to a sleek fitting pair of black slacks with a black top, beaded collar, and cuffs. Then downstairs to dinner. She'd finish *The Da Vinci Code* when she came back up.

Peggy ushered her to the same table-for-two she had had last week. She felt comfortable here. The aroma of roasted prime rib with garlic seasoning wafted through the room. *I am starving,* she thought, not having eaten since morning. *I am getting food.* Two before her in line made it no wait at all. Her turn. She looked through several slices Peggy's chef had already carved. She'd take medium rare before she'd slice her own and splatter her clothes.

"Fussy, aren't we," the voice said in her ear, startling her. The meat left the serving fork and dropped onto the platter, splashing juices over her sleeve. Thank goodness her outfit was black.

"You startled me, and look, I stained my clothes. Why did you come up behind me like that?" She said, grabbing an extra napkin to wipe her sleeve.

Wade grinned and apologized. "Sorry your clothes got stained. I wanted to get your attention."

"You succeeded," she replied, "but you weren't supposed to be here until tomorrow. What made you come early?"

He looked surprised. "How did you know that?"

She seemed a bit embarrassed. "When I booked my room yesterday, Peggy told me you'd be up Saturday."

"That's odd," he said. "She called me yesterday evening and told me my room was available a day early. 'Come up a day early and rest. Prime rib is on the menu for tomorrow's dinner.' Now why would she say that?"

Stevie shrugged, then blushed, realizing Peggy might be playing Cupid, not something she was ready for.

"So why are you here, after one week, when the pad won't be laid for another three?"

Come clean, she thought. "I was hoping to see you. I wanted to apologize for prying into your past, and for being rather obnoxious. It was thoughtless."

He motioned to the buffet. "Let's get our dinner and talk."

Surprisingly, they were both ravenous. Little conversation passed between them as they enjoyed their meal, except for Wade telling her he had thought about her statements and had done a little research on his lineage.

"What about your parents? Would they know the family's lineage?"

He shook his head. "Dad died in '96; Mom a few years ago."

"I'm sorry, Wade. That must have hurt."

He nodded. "It did, very much, but there are things that have hurt worse." He shook it off. "I did, however, ask Peggy. She's local. She knows an elderly man who remembered the McFadden name. He didn't remember much, only that a controversy had split the town before the second World War. McFadden sold his land to his sister, my great grandmother, who married William Patrick Henderson, the initials on the strongbox."

"That's a good start."

"It is, and there's a bit more. According to this octogenarian, the McFadden side of the family left for North Carolina, never coming back, not even one visit. That's all he knew, but for me, that's significant."

"It sure is." She considered her next question. "Someday, would you want to find them?"

He motioned his hand yes or no. "That's a long shot, but I'm certain it had something to do with the Federal Reserve, because my great grandfather not only opposed that banking cartel, he gave a passionate speech against them and the Board of Directors, passionate enough to cause dissention in the party and the county, and, supposedly, there were a few attempts on his life."

"We must have read similar articles," Stevie replied, "because I found that speech. I printed it but haven't read it yet; just skimmed a little. I'll read the whole thing when I have quiet time, but the section I saw was where he brings charges against the Fed's Board of Governors and a few other politicos for conspiracy and treason. Strong charges."

"If his charges were true, and I believe they were because he knew finance, this private corporation we call the Fed pulled a fast one on Congress and the people back in 1913. But what's the significance of the note? What did my grandfather expect from the person who discovered that strongbox?"

Stevie shrugged. "Can't figure that out." She thought a few moments. "Have you read, *The Creature from Jekyll Island*? It's a book about the Federal Reserve."

Wade shook his head. "It has kind of a Syfy name, but no, I don't recall that title. I assume you have?"

Stevie nodded. "Partially. It's over six hundred pages of information about money and history of the Fed. It doesn't give a pretty picture of this banking cartel or our government."

"I wouldn't expect an English major relaxing in the evening and sipping tea with a book like that. *Pride and Prejudice, Gone with the Wind,* maybe Michener's *Hawaii,* but a book like that? Why would you read that?"

"You'd be surprised what this English major has read, and that book is not at all dry. In fact, it's fascinating. I read all the summaries and a few chapters that drew me in. I have to read more, but what I found most interesting was that the Fed contributed to bankrupting our country and that it exercised control over our government by 'owning' our politicians, then and more today.

"That's where I see a connection with your grandfather's speech and the note. Remember, when he gave that speech, we were in the middle of the Great Depression. People, families, were suffering, starving, losing everything they had. What if it were because of the Fed?"

He shrugged. "Meaning?"

"Meaning the Fed created money and expanded the monetary system by a nuanced definition of an asset. Being an English major," she gave a wry smile, "I don't fully understand it. At first I confused it with buying on margin - you invest in something, putting down a tiny percent and borrow the rest, but that's not banks creating assets. The bank's Fractional Reserves policy creates those. You deposit $1,000, the bank claims $1,000 as an asset but holds maybe 10%. It lends the remainder but still records $1,000 as an asset and the cycle continues. So the Fed always lends more than it actually has, and buys with money that's not really there. That about ends my understanding of money, except I know this cycle creates debt, inflation or recession, and that borrowing, and debt, doesn't stop. Notice another thing, politicians don't stop it, either, maybe for political reasons." She shrugged. "Who knows?"

"It's possible, Stevie, but seriously, to tie all that in with owning the country? I don't see it. I own my own business. I work with architects who design golf courses and shopping courts in the south, or wherever the clientele will pick up and go. Lots of money in this business, but neither I nor the people I work with have given any indication that they believe the Federal Reserve controls our government. Conversation focuses on borrowing money: interest rates rising," he pointed upwards with his fork, "or falling." His fork did a nosedive.

"You seem nonchalant about this."

"Why not, since I don't see a connection, and I can't control a thing the Fed does."

She let it go. "But since your great-grandfather's speech was given during the Great Depression, he probably believed their monetary policies had caused that crash, something they claimed they could prevent when they presented their case to the government in 1913."

She inhaled deeply, remembering the day she got her 9-11 story and what she had witnessed. Is it possible our government and big money had something to do with it? That cataclysm had given the government lots more control over its citizens and their privacy, writing off

Constitutional rights. Her reaction to the government's conclusions indicated whitewash. She shut her eyes so she could block out images of bloody bodies covered with soot, emerging from collapsed buildings. After inhaling dust from pulverized concrete and cinder blocks, their lungs had given out. They had died on route to the hospital.

Stevie had ended her story with the woman's last words, "Tell my husband I love him." She had choked back tears as she had written that, and it had taken weeks to push that image from her mind.

She had lived through her father's death, and if she faced reality, she had never fully recovered. She had also seen lives destroyed when Samir, her mother's student at the academy, was pushed off the roof by his father-in-law who hated his son-in-law because he was a Muslim and had married his daughter. But Stevie had never witnessed their deaths, been by their side while life's spirit faded; she had never heard their dying words. But with this woman, Stevie had been there. She had seen individual and total devastation.

Finally, after months agonizing over a cataclysmic disaster she could not control, she had blocked it out; she didn't want to relive it now. However, from that moment, she believed the connection between government, wars, money, the Fed, were connected big time. That's when she read *The Creature from Jekyll Island,* one book, among others, that confirmed her suspicion.

But Wade didn't see it nor did anyone she talked to, including her editor. "No," he had said when she had broached the topic several years ago, "I am not giving you liberty and time for some wild goose chase to research the Fed and some conspiracy." So that ended that, but Stevie never stopped believing there was a strong connection, and Wade's strongbox and that note convinced her even more.

"Who owns us?" WPH had buried that box for a reason. Was it to research McFadden and realize he was right about the Fed bankrupting the country? Was it to warn us another Great Depression, or worse, had to occur someday, or was it to reconnect family, to find out what happened and make it right? She sighed. Enough. These thoughts could wait for another day.

What she wanted now was to continue the evening as it had been going. She had had her share of dating since her early twenties, but aside from parting as friends, or not, no man had been as interesting as Wade, except Mason. There was always Mason, but despite his telling her he would always be there for her, he hadn't been around in years. Sadly for her, he had recently gotten engaged.

Tonight was a serendipitous evening she didn't want to end. Like all of us, she was a cog in the wheel of life, completely incapable of changing anything, which made her determined to live in the present. She changed the subject.

"I'm glad you arrived a day early because I'm enjoying the evening immensely," she heard herself say. *Where did those words come from? Who was that person who had just spoken?* Somewhat bewildered with her candor, she continued, "This topic can wait till another time. Right now, I have to respond quickly to stave off my coffee and sugar addiction," she pushed her seat back and got up. "I'm getting coffee and dessert. Care to join me?"

She was the most spontaneous person Wade had ever met since . . . . He shook it off. He had no idea what Stevie had intended to say, but he was glad she wanted to close the McFadden topic. These revelations about his family were too much. His drawback at the moment was in not knowing what to do or say in the presence of a woman. It had been so long.

Fortunately, when Peggy related the entire menu to him yesterday, she had included desserts. He wasn't going to miss pecan pie, German apple cake and something he never thought he'd see even fifty miles from the City, tiramisu. If Stevie was going for dessert, he was too. He pushed back his chair and followed her.

8

THE FRACKING SITE

Last night's dinner had ended on a very amiable note. They had continued the evening in the sunroom, an all glass addition that overlooked woodlands and a lake, whose ceiling presented a view of a starry sky, reminding her of skies at the Manasquan shore years ago. By 11:00, having had two glasses of wine, and having planned a morning at the fracking site, they had gone to their rooms thinking pleasant thoughts about each other.

Early next day, after another delicious breakfast which they ate together at the same table – 'their' table, as they were now calling it - they drove to the fracking site in Wade's SUV, a black Mercedes M-Class, as he described it, which meant nothing to Stevie, who only had her Buick at the behest of her stepfather's generosity. Had he and her mom not married, Stevie would have been driving a used something or other.

The morning welcomed them, strutting its early pageantry of budding leaves and flowers, accentuated with a dreamy breeze. Windows down, Stevie was enjoying the drive as much as she had enjoyed dinner. She didn't want to hold on too tightly though, thinking of Cinderella and fantasies that ended at midnight. Surprisingly, Wade seemed as happy as she did, turning on a radio station that picked up with Lionel Richie's "All Night Long."

"Great beat, great sound." Her shoulders moved with its Caribbean beat.

"You like 80's music?"

"Put on Michael Jackson and you'll have to stop the car." She smiled and in that second, Wade forgot his hurt.

They arrived at the fracking site too soon for Stevie. She could have driven for hours. Sometimes on a long drive, "Running on Empty," would surface from deep in her soul, and she'd want to drive, from nowhere to nowhere, urged on by a feeling of sadness she would not identify. She brought herself back to reality and focused on their objective.

They arrived at the fracking site, pleasantly surprised by what they saw. The weather was clear, sun bright, and the job was progressing faster than either of them had expected. Except for one small strip that remained open to let in workers and materials, the form work was completed. Dump trucks filled with sand followed each other in one steady stream. Each pulled up to the nascent site pad, raised its bed, dumped its contents, lowered its bed and left for another load while little skid steers hurried about like busy ants, biting into the sand piles and putting its load where it was most needed. Then, back, and forth, they leveled the layers. The hilly, hard terrain had been leveled in a week. Frank must have had double crews working non-stop to get this done. He was ahead of schedule.

"We are way ahead of schedule," he announced with great satisfaction, forcing himself not to succumb to a smile. "Give me two more weeks and you can come up for your fracking story. You'll see the liners laid, gravel and sand hard-packed for the pad, trucks, pumps, drilling, and reclamation wells for reclaiming water used to frack the shale. The process is safe; you'll see that too, Ms. Komsky, but I'm sure you'll get several perspectives on that." He knew Stevie wouldn't accept his statement without checking other sources.

"Roads. What about roads?" Stevie asked, against a backdrop of grinding gears and monster motors. "I've seen huge trucks on local roads, and I'm wondering if these country roads can handle them. These trucks are imposing, and tankers that'll follow will most likely be bigger."

"Good question, Ms. Komsky. You're correct. Most local roads could not handle that much weight; so Best Energy reinforced existing roads that had potential, or built new roads wherever needed. A few start off Route 6. Notice them on your way out." Had he allowed himself to be anything other than all business, he would have lost his composure. For some inexplicable reason, her image still lingered from her first visit.

For Stevie, she wondered if Mr. Frank Goring was capable of a smile. There had to be one somewhere. But his explanations about the site satisfied her, and that's what she was here for. The company was taking all precautions to make the area and roads safe. She would continue to talk to locals and was still concerned about reclamation wells, wondering if seepage would bleed into the county's water supply.

As Frank conversed with Wade about the lay of the land and the horizontal distance Frank expected to be drilling, Stevie snapped a few pictures and walked the perimeter of what would soon be the construction pad. She loved the outdoors in spring and fall, clunking around in heavy boots, jeans, and layers of flannel. She loved the swoosh of leaves during the day, the sky at night, and she loved the ocean, what she missed most since her mom married her stepdad almost twenty years ago, moving her from Manasquan to Princeton's suburbs.

She missed long walks in the surf, crashing waves of an angry sea, seagulls, and pelicans diving for food. She missed searching for unique shells and watching hermit crabs dig their way into a sandy refuge, and she loved sitting on their back porch in their tiny home in Manasquan, watching a starry sky. Her mom would point to constellations she remembered from younger days and explain the myths behind them.

Most of all, Stevie missed her dad. She relived images of him lifting her to his shoulders, spraying up foam and ocean as he ran through the surf. She'd hold on and squeal, but she always felt safe with her dad, and then he was gone, taken from them in a war, a UN peacekeeping force in Lebanon to contain a civil war after Israel invaded. Invaded and invaded . . . a country that kept invading, that we kept defending, which allowed it to keep invading.

Wow, how had she gone from point A to point Z from a wisp of a memory about loving the outdoors? She glanced up. Wade had ended his conversation with Frank and was walking towards her with a captivating smile.

"Hey, Stevie, it's a beautiful day. Want to walk in the woods; then grab lunch?"

A walk in the woods? No one had ever invited her do that, but for whatever reason, it seemed like the perfect thing to do and the perfect person to do it with.

9

STORIES SHE COULD NOT COVER

Stevie left Monday morning's staff briefing not particularly interested in topics Jeff wanted covered. One or two might work, but nothing intriguing.

"Come up with something better," he said. "I'll consider it."

There was a little freedom in that and she'd give it some thought, but her mind was focused elsewhere. To be specific, it was focused on Bradford County, Pennsylvania and it had nothing to do with fracking, McFadden, or packs of United States Treasury Notes, and only a little to do with an aloof fracking commander who refused to smile.

What occupied her thoughts most was Wade. After a wonderful weekend with him, she couldn't keep her mind on much else. About six feet, four inches of muscle, dark black hair and jet black eyes, with a smile that melted into soft curls at each end, he was very easy to look at, and after two days of conversation about nothing too personal, she found herself wanting to know more. First and foremost, was he single, married, a little of both? Secondly, why did he lapse into periodic fugues of melancholy and did it matter?

Shaking herself back to reality, she reviewed the week's assignments: the president's trip to India – boring; the Democrat's NY gubernatorial primary coming up in a week – possibilities, and the consequences of free, democratic elections in Gaza this past January. Our president insists Hamas be on the ballot. Hamas wins, Israel embargos Palestine, as if conditions in Gaza weren't bad enough, and the secretary of state says we didn't realize Hamas would be so strong at the ballot box. Sure. Stevie wasn't going to write that one, not following the accepted narrative, and she doubted Jeff would let her stray from it.

The next option was a follow-up article on the progress of the Iraqi War. She wasn't doing that one either. Depending upon what group was doing the survey, data ranged between 35,000 to hundreds of thousands of Iraqi civilians and over 4,000 American soldiers killed. She turned her back on this one too. Writing about lives destroyed in Iraq, soldiers who'd never see spouses or children again, or come home to another Christmas was not for her. She did not want to write about something she had lived.

The final option: construction of the 1,776 foot-tall Freedom Tower for the new World Trade center. Groundbreaking was scheduled for July 4. All the who's who would be there. She could get interested in that, especially since she had covered the one-year memorial of

9-11. As much as she'd hate to relive those memories, the topic was relevant. But early July? She could circumnavigate the globe in a river cruiser and have plenty of time for that. She'd take it, but she'd need topics for the present. She'd take the Democrat primary, but if she couldn't come up with something for another article Jeffrey would approve, she'd be working in the mail room.

Maybe with a little persuasion, he'd let her write an article that addressed deeper issues in the Middle East that didn't genuflect to Israel or spout the accepted mantra. Maybe she could dissect "Operation Clean Break." That was a thought. She could relate that in some way to Gaza elections and the progress of the Iraqi war, and there'd be no need for an opinion on that; the document said it all. She only had to present it. Like it or hate it, most readers would be able to consider the implications for themselves. Would Jeffrey give her the go-ahead? She'd ask

10

WADE'S REACTION

Three weeks passed. The assignments she had submitted to Jeff were, according to him, outstanding. "Stellar" was the word he had used. She had covered the primary and done an introductory piece on November's gubernatorial election, each candidate's platform, campaign strategy and a brief profile. That took more research and interviewing than she had anticipated, but she had met some interesting people, which would lead to an easier follow-up after the election.

She had approached Jeffrey about "Operation Clean Break" last week, had given him an outline of what the paper presented and surprisingly, he had given her the go-ahead. Basically, the Clean Break plan suggested Israel discard the land for peace concept, make a clean break, and eliminate any Middle Eastern state that would conflict with Israel's acquisition of land for the "Greater Israel." Ironic that it was written for Israel's prime minister in 1996 by American officials in high government positions whose allegiance seemed to be Israel first. It didn't matter that American servicemen would be doing the grunt work, dying, or coming back mutilated.

When she had presented the topic to Jeff, she was convinced he would reject it, but he didn't. She had sanitized it, no politics, no diatribe, just a clean dissection exactly as it had been written, tying in a few lines about PNAC, the Project for the New American Century, which recommended a new geo-strategy to start wars and change governments. Not a pretty picture, but no one could challenge that either since it was all documented.

Her stories done, she had left work early and was heading to Pennsylvania, this time with an invitation from Wade Henderson himself. He had gotten her number from Peggy and was eager to tell her the pad was complete and trucks were rolling on in. As she drove, she felt a surge of excitement and anticipation; she would be seeing Wade and the fracking site, and although the fracking story had been her objective, she was more excited to see Wade.

Despite this being only her third trip, Polly's parking lot seemed like familiar territory. She pulled her Buick into a space two away from the wide staircase that led to a wrap-around porch. Déjà vu, she grabbed her suitcase from the trunk, hoisted it up and through the front door and was greeted by Peggy in the foyer, who had decorated for Palm Sunday and Easter. Pastel blues, pinks, and greens, with Easter bunny figurines, had replaced the leprechauns from St. Patrick's Day. Delightful. Peggy escorted her to the same room she had had twice before, beaming all the way.

"He's here," she said softly as they walked up the wide staircase to Stevie's room.

44

"Already?" Stevie asked.

Peggy smiled. "See you at dinner," then she left for other responsibilities. Being manager of Polly's made her a factotum at the inn. She could do it all.

Stevie had no time to relax. Her cell phone read, "Wade H. Hurry down. Trucks r in; Frank's been drilling first well for 2 days. If we hurry, might catch last of that & everything else first hand - drilling, casings, pouring cement . . . ."

Stevie splashed water on her face, put on a casual pair of jeans, work shoes, and a cotton, long-sleeve sweater, Wedgewood blue and white, cable knit. The blue intensified her eyes. Then she dusted a hint of makeup on her face and dashed to the foyer where Wade was waiting, promising her he'd get her back in time for Peggy's dinner. That gave them less than two hours. They'd never make it.

Thirty minutes later, they were on the construction pad, loaded with trucks holding water, sand and lubricating fluid, side-stepping pipes that connected all this to the well that was being bored.

Frank was overseeing every detail. When he saw Wade and Stevie, he left his team to meet them. In a gesture of courtesy that surprised Stevie, Frank held out his hand for her as she stepped over huge pipes and couplings. "We began drilling this week, drilled about a mile down, way below the drinking water level. We're at the kick-off point and are beginning the horizontal phase. We'll drill about a mile and a half into that; then we'll send down the steel pipes, casings. After that, we'll send down cement to secure the casings in place. That will create a protective barrier for the aquifers. Don't believe we'll get to that this weekend, but we may. We're progressing just

45

fine; in fact, we're ahead of schedule," a fact which pleased him, because he looked directly into her eyes and smiled, a genuine yet sensual smile that made her stomach lurch. *Woah, where did that come from?*

Stevie was awed, first by Frank's smile and its intensity, then by the complexity of so many pipes leading from and going to trucks and the drilled site. This was a good story for her; she loved intricate detail and close examination of how things worked. For a second, her thoughts turned to the steel box and "McFadden" painted on a rock. That required close examination too. Maybe she'd be following that story in the future, but later for that. Here and now was her primary story.

She and Wade stayed longer than anticipated. In a bit, the sun would be heading for the horizon, and Peggy's staff would be clearing the buffet. If Peggy weren't saving them a plate, they'd be raiding her fridge when they got back.

They continued conversing with Frank and Gary about everything and Stevie snapped a few last photos. Winding down the fracking formalities, Frank asked about the strongbox and if it had taken on more meaning.

Stevie shook her head. "Just a lot more questions without answers. But we've researched McFadden and how he's tied to the Federal Reserve. He made some – no, made a *lot* of enemies because he told the truth about our banking system, about which most people today know nothing."

"You mean how the Fed controls our government?" Gary interjected without emotion.

Stevie gulped and looked at Wade, who tried to avoid Gary's comment. He, a man in business, highly educated in that field, hesitated to connect the Fed with government control while Gary, a fracker whose education was most likely mechanical engineering, put the two together like summer sun and heat.

"Why do you say that?" Wade asked.

"Say what? That the Fed controls our government? Of course it does. Anybody who controls a country's money supply controls its government. A Rothschild said that a long time ago, and it's true."

That comment shocked Stevie. How would Gary know about the Fed, government control and a Rothschild?

"You've read about this topic?" She asked, looking at Gary and Frank.

Frank nodded; Gary replied. "You think we'd have all this national debt if the Fed had governmental constraints, or an independent audit, or we had stayed on a gold standard? You'll never get those though, because the Fed controls the government, and wars. Who wins from that? Government and big bankers." His countenance became grave with a hint of anger. "Not our troops who come home mutilated," he turned away, "or don't come home at all."

Stevie hesitated; then asked. "Personal experience?"

"If you call losing a nephew personal experience, then yes." Gary pulled up a feeder pipe "Iraqi War: 9-11 let our government justify anything. Wouldn't surprise me if we let the damn Arabs bomb those towers." His face bore a sinister look. "But then I'd be called a conspiracy theorist."

Suddenly Stevie was four again, and military brass and a chaplain were knocking on her mother's door. Her mom was sinking to the floor, shrieking hysterically, with Stevie glued to her leg. She knew what it had been like for Gary's family to have received that news.

No . . . I'm not reliving this, not now. She shook herself out of her past and looked for Wade hoping he'd agree to go. His face was ashen white. Without a word, he headed to his truck.

11

HAMILTON PARK

A cool breeze blew off the Hudson. Stevie didn't mind; she actually welcomed it. She had worn a light jacket and found the evening air refreshing. She had come here to her bench in Hamilton Park on the other side of the Hudson, the place New Yorkers called the sixth borough, to gaze at the New York skyline, the best light show in the world. Even though she could see the skyline from her porch, this was her perfect place to think. She sat back and reflected on anything, sometimes nothing, while gazing at the night sky, the lights of New York, and the Chrysler Building, the Empire State and what would soon be the new home for the New York Times.

Wade's reaction to Gary's comment was still bothering her. Unwittingly, Gary had triggered an immediate change in him. Although Stevie had seen hints of melancholy and depression once or twice, even anger in Wade, he had stayed connected, but from the moment

Gary mentioned big bankers, government control, 9-11, and the Iraqi war, Wade was a different man, quiet, introspective, reticent. He functioned robotically; he wasn't there, and all Stevie's attempts to pull him back failed. This morning, she had packed up and left without a goodbye.

Peggy had pleaded with her to stay. "He'll come around," she had said, over and over. "Stay at least for breakfast." But Stevie was adamant. Something deep was troubling Wade, that was obvious, and Stevie could not make it better. Leaving was the best option at this point.

"He's had a tough time these past few years," Peggy confided as she walked Stevie to her car. "Don't be too hard on him. He really doesn't know how to fix this."

Stevie nodded. She'd never pry; never ask why, but she couldn't stay. She accepted two biscuits and a huge raisin scone Peggy insisted she take, and left.

Her drive home was depressing. She liked Wade a lot, maybe too much. He was intelligent yet down to earth, industrious, amenable, helpful, willing to pick up a wrench and help Gary secure a connection, and ready to absorb all the details Frank explained. He also loved being outdoors and appreciated a nighttime sky, but something was eating at him.

She understood the nature of shutting feelings inside and shutting people out. Her mother had first-hand experience with that. Hell, if she had been honest with herself, she'd admit she had been doing that too, same as Wade.

Gary's mention of war had changed Wade instantly. In his mid-thirties, that could have meant the Gulf War in '91 or the Iraqi Invasion in 2003. But he was too old for the

Iraqi invasion three years ago and it was fifteen years since the Gulf War.

What else? An accident? But that wouldn't be a war, unless . . . unless it was an accident or a death from a war, or something as bad. Gary had mentioned 9-11; Peggy had said "these past few years." "Past few years," she uttered. Could it have been . . . 9-11? She shuddered, praying she was wrong. Should she ask? No, it was not something she wanted to know.

12

WADE'S WEST POINT PAST

Wade's countenance dissolved when he realized Stevie had gone. What a fool he had been. He could have kicked himself. He had let his nightmares affect the only person he had warmed to in five years, and he had driven her away. A stupid, stupid fool.

But Peggy was right; he didn't know how to fix this. He was caught between his personal tragedy, denying reality, and falling back on years of training.

From the time he was eight & his parents moved to New York, his path had seemed clear, never a question asked. His parents had begun investing in real estate in the tri-state area decades ago when markets were depressed. Once in New York, with lots of extra money from the sale of their house, acres of land, and a horse farm, places in New Jersey like Franklin Lakes, Ridgewood, Englewood Cliffs, Long Beach Island proved excellent investments, as did depressed businesses and stocks, mostly tech stocks and pharmaceuticals. When markets took off, they had become multi-millionaires, tipping the billion mark.

What this meant for Wade was that he'd never see a day of public school for his secondary education. His parents researched the best private academies in New York and surrounding areas. Because of proximity and reputation, they selected a private academy in Dobbs Ferry, a perfect fit for Wade.

The only thing they had not considered was that, for the kid who had become addicted to Dungeons and Dragons, and Risk at an early age, and who would take every opportunity to visit West Point so close to Dobbs Ferry, their son would choose a military academy.

When Wade announced he had applied for admission, his parents were shocked. He could have chosen any Ivy League school; he could have studied abroad; he could have named his school, yet he chose military.

With an outstanding GPA, and his father having rubbed elbows with New York officials, his appointment was secure, but after his first few months as a plebe, he wasn't so sure he was. It was grueling.

Never a quitter, he stuck it out. By his junior year, his 'cow' year, he had earned the respect of his classmates in the classroom, and his teammates on the football field. With his peers, he had earned the distinction of having broken quite a few rules without ever having gotten caught. Wade Henderson had never walked an area tour.

No matter what prank he played, what rules he sidestepped, Wade had never gotten caught. His secret was keeping a secret. He didn't need accolades, even when he and his buddies replicated MacArthur's supposed prank and, in the middle of the night moved the reveille wake-up cannon to the top of the clock tower. Impossible. Yet, in the morning, it was up there, without a clue as to how or who.

But a military education demands honesty and loyalty to the point of indoctrination, indoctrination to follow orders and swear fealty to your country regardless of evidence that challenges that loyalty. Dishonorable acts perpetrated by your country were inconceivable, but 9-11 challenged Wade's loyalty in a way he had never thought anything could.

Wade's internal conflict regarding 9-11 was questioning our government's beforehand knowledge. But, believing that labeled you a conspiracy theorist, despite empirical data that proved your theory right. However, since any accusation that our government knew about the attack would be considered disloyal, maybe treasonous, Wade refused to see through his programming.

Despite degrees in engineering and business, Wade accepted his government's conclusions; he had to, to justify the attack by terrorists that took the life of his wife and child.

This was the nightmare he had lived with for five years. He was unable to discuss it, sometimes barely able to get through the day. Night brought sweats and phantasmagoric illusions. At times, he imagined he was going insane; he'd call out for Debbie, but she wasn't there. No Debbie, no Ryan. They would never be there. He didn't want to live fifty more years without them; he didn't want to live another day.

With Gary's comment, these memories and contradictions surfaced, and as much as he wanted to be with Stevie, the first time he wanted to be with anybody since losing Debbie, he could not pull himself out of the maelstrom that was sucking him down.

He forced himself back to reality, chastising himself for having been crude and insensitive to Stevie. He'd apologize, let her know it wasn't her, just him, a middle-aged man who didn't care if he ever grew old.

13

HOME FOR EASTER

The day before Easter, April 15, and Stevie was on her way to Princeton, her home since she was ten. Greeted at the door by her mom's giant "pull-away-from" hugs and kisses, and a warm hug from her step dad, Vaughn Otis/Barrett, Stevie realized she had stayed away too long. Why come home only for special days and events? Her family was too important for her to put them second or third on her most significant list.

Next, she hugged Hillary, Vaughn's sister-in-law who had divorced Vaughn's brother eighteen years ago. The divorce was justifiable beyond question. Hillary had never been able to conceive, but she became baby Samir's surrogate mother when Rachel began Princeton a month after Samir was born, eighteen years ago. Hillary would always be part of Vaughn & Cassie's family.

Parker, Stevie's stepbrother, came in from the kitchen and wrapped his arms around her. Rachel, married to

Parker for a decade and very pregnant with baby number two, was right beside him. This family unit was more than family; they were inextricably linked by a devastating tragedy none of them would ever forget, and it made them stronger, one cohesive unit against hardship.

Parker junior, eight, nicknamed Sonny, danced around his mother's legs kicking a soccer ball.

"Outside with that, or you'll lose it," Parker said, definitely a father image. "You trip your mother and she'll get hurt." Stevie hugged them all, Sonny first, before he picked up his ball and headed outside.

Her half-brother and sister, twins, came tumbling in from the game room or the entertainment room, or maybe the bowling alley. Who knows what they had chosen for entertainment. Vaughn's mansion had it all. Travis, older by three minutes, and Julia, recently turned nineteen, were effusive with excitement to see their sister again. They surrounded her with hugs and affection and questions about her lifestyle in Manhattan as if something had changed since they had last seen her New Year's Day.

"I've been working in New York almost five years. What's all the fuss about now?" She paused. "Wait one minute." She looked down. "Julia . . . what do you call these?"

Stevie poked her finger into huge holes in her sister's jeans. "Did you buy these this way, or did you let them rot for ten years?"

Julia laughed. "This is the style Sis!"

Stevie turned to her mother. "And you *let* her wear these things? If these tears were any higher, her underwear would be showing!"

"I'm nineteen, Stevie. I can wear what I want!" She flipped her head back defiantly, sending a mane of blond hair flying behind her."

Cassie shook her head. "No she can't, not as long as I'm paying for it and she's living in our house. The jeans were a compromise. We agreed to torn jeans a tiny bit below the waist, but none of this three inches below the navel."

"Don't let me see you wearing slutty clothes," Stevie admonished. "You want to attract a guy, do it with your looks and your brains." Stevie looked her in the eye. "Agreed?"

Julia nodded reluctantly, but she got the point, then took the topic back to where Stevie had interrupted her. "Anything new happening in and around Manhattan? I'm so much more cosmopolitan now." she spun her hand in the air.

Stevie chuckled. At fourteen, they had viewed their sister's life as "blah." Five years later, they, especially Julia, had recycled their sister into a bon vivant. Wow, were they wrong.

"Okay, later, you can ask me about my dull life in New York, but right now, someone is missing. Where's Samir?"

She scanned the great room, the huge foyer with its spiral staircases, walked down the hall to the kitchen to ask Sarah, and back. Still no Sam. "Where is he Rachel?"

His mother smiled. "He wants to make a grand entrance."

Stevie was ten when Sammy was born. Because like her, he had lost his father, she bonded with him at first sight, while he was still in neonatal, and she doted on him whenever her mother stayed at Hillary's townhouse, the complex where Rachel lived after her husband, Samir, had been killed. Sam grew up with Stevie as a concomitant in his life.

Finally, that strikingly handsome face appeared. "Aunt Stevie," he said in his mellow voice, open arms and his charming smile lighting up his face, making his dark olive-shaped eyes twinkle.

Stevie hugged him tightly, not wanting to let go. "So now you need a grand entrance?"

He smiled. He looked so much like his father. Stevie wondered how Rachel dealt with the constant memory of her dead husband, pushed off the dorm-roof eighteen years ago by her father. Did it bother Parker, Vaughn's son, who had loved Rachel since their academy days, when she had unequivocally chosen Samir?

Those days seemed so long ago, yet here they were; her mother Cassie, married to Vaughn, the man she had once hated; Hillary, an integral part of the family even without her ex-husband, and Parker married to Rachel. How does time work, this thing that morphs one day into another so seamlessly you never even notice, until suddenly, you look back, almost nineteen years have passed, and you're getting old.

For Stevie, she saw this in her mom, the touch of gray around her hairline and her shoulder-length dirty blond hair. Her mom was still as beautiful as she was when she had been younger, but little lines had formed around her mouth and eyes. Inevitable.

She saw age creeping into her own life. She was no longer the four-year-old who clung to her mother after her father had died, or the nine-year-old her mother had pulled from Manasquan to teach at an academy near Princeton to forget her pain. She was twenty-eight, a mature woman, perfectly capable of living life on her own, wondering why she was always alone.

Enough of that. She was with her family whom she hadn't seen since Christmas break, or "winter break" as the secular revisionists now called it, and Travis and Julia were asking one question after another about everything, like shooting pellets from a BB gun, as though they hadn't been to New York dozens of times and hadn't saved every issue of the paper when it had run Stevie's stories.

Sarah entered to announce appetizers were being served in the lodge, Cassie's favorite room. Arm in arm, hand in hand, the family strolled to the lodge, a huge room on the left side of the mansion, with its all-glass, back wall overlooking an Olympic-sized pool, cabanas, acres of gardens and stables, far back so they couldn't be seen. It was a spectacular setting, a beautiful view - peaceful, serene, a section of the mansion reserved for quiet time that boasted its own entrance and underground parking for extra privacy.

Amidst the glitz and trappings of the other rooms, the lodge was designed to replicate the foyer of an exclusive ski lodge and it surpassed anything Cassie had seen. Despite its size, warm shades of brown gave it an ambiance of comfort and the wall to wall, floor to ceiling rich brown stone fireplace could light the room and penetrate her heart. It was as welcoming today as it had been years before when Cassie was first here with her class the night after graduation from Chelsea academy; the night they had all been together for the last time, without Samir.

Cassie settled into her favorite recliner with Vaughn at her side. At one end of the room, Sarah and staff had set up a delicious buffet: clams on the half-shell, shrimp, lobster tails, chunks of ham, cheese wedges, beefsteak, olives, breads, salads, all kinds of condiments.

"Don't bother with dinner, Sarah," Cassie smiled. "This will be quite enough."

Love was the key ingredient in that room. Despite the food, dinner that went half eaten and luscious desserts, Stevie was so overwhelmed to be home with her brothers & sister she almost cried.

In the evening, Sarah set up coffee, tea, aperitifs and brought most of the desserts from the dining room back to the lodge. Conversation still flowed, and Sonny was forced to sit still, difficult for an eight-year-old. Now, Stevie mentioned her latest story and her encounters with a businessman named Wade Henderson. Sam was intrigued by the 'X' and the McFadden name on the rock, but the strong box filled with two-dollar bills, U.S. Treasury Notes, intrigued Cassie.

"Sounds like a Federal Reserve connection to Kennedy's assassination," she said. Cassie had researched big money, the Rothschilds and government control for decades, and believed a Zionist connection existed among all three as far back as Balfour's Declaration, The Federal Reserve, and World War I. She couldn't prove it, but 9-11 had convinced her.

She believed Israel had known about the attack. Could it send five reporters to cover it if it hadn't, hadn't known something no one else knew, or admitted to knowing? And why would these five Israeli reporters disguise themselves as Arabs while covering this secret, *surprise* attack from

61

the NJ side of the Hudson? And why celebrate as the WTC towers came down?

The conversation went back and forth with question after question about the 9-11 attack or using the two-dollar bills in some way to prove Kennedy's assassination. Sam was becoming increasingly agitated, knowing why his father had been killed, when Mason, Parker's best friend since day one at Chelsea Academy, walked in, hand in hand with his fiancé of two months, and conversation ceased. Not expecting to see Stevie, Mason came to an abrupt halt and froze.

"Stevie, hi; what are you doing here?"

She gave him a quizzical look. "My family lives here. Where else would I be the day before Easter?"

"Of course. I didn't mean it that way. I just didn't expect to see you here. Parker invited me – us." He looked at his fiancé, then glanced around the room. "Remember the last time we were all in this room?"

"No Mason, I wasn't here when my mom's Shakespeare class met for the last time after graduation. I was ten."

Mason blushed, his face matching his red hair, then introduced his fiancé. "Patricia, my fiancé. You've never met. She's my dental assistant."

Well, thought Stevie, that's one way to marry a dentist. "Nice to meet you, Patricia." Stevie got up and extended her hand.

Patricia was short, athletically built, dark hair, dark eyes, the opposite of Stevie.

"Excuse my manners," Stevie offered. "Please, come, sit. Guess you know everybody here?" She glanced at Patricia.

"She met your mom and dad and everybody else at the engagement party. You missed it."

"I'm sorry, I tried to get back, but I was covering a story in upstate New York and my primary source could only meet me that day. But I'll be there for the wedding, hopefully, whenever that is."

"No date yet. We've got time."

Stevie nodded and ushered them forward. By now everyone was standing and walking towards the new arrivals. The couple was greeted affectionately by all, especially Parker, who loved talking about old times with his buddy and favorite receiver, as if they could recapture their football days by talking about them.

They got comfortable, accepted martinis, and turned the discussion to weddings and bridal showers. Travis, Julia, and Sam left quietly; Sonny left, kicking his ball.

Stevie followed, escaping to the kitchen, and began helping Sarah. "Had enough of family already?" Sarah teased.

Stevie laughed and shook her head. I'll join the younger set. I fall somewhere in the middle – way past college but still single."

Sarah's countenance took a down turn. "Oh, Honey, ignore Mason. He's a jerk."

"Seems I've met a lot of them in my 'young' lifetime." She put a few shrimp on a plate for nibbles, and pointed in the direction of the game room "Downstairs?"

Sarah nodded, indicating that was the way Stevie's siblings, Sam, and the soccer fanatic had gone. Stevie followed, emptiness in her heart, wondering what part of her personality rejected commitment, and why? Maybe someday she'd have the courage to face it.

14

MASON'S UNEXPECTED
PASS

Around 11:30, her mother and Vaughn retired for the night. The younger group stayed in the game room leaving Parker, Rachel, and Mason in the lodge to reminisce about old times. Patricia listened. Stevie had come up to join them, but again, did not fit in. She took a giant mug of tea to the gazebo Vaughn had built for her when she and her mom had moved in. Vaughn's mansion was opulent in every way, but it wasn't what Stevie could adjust to at ten.

She had needed a quiet place, a place of her own apart from her palatial room, somewhere outside so she could be part of nature surrounded by foliage; listen to crickets chirp without being eaten alive by mosquitoes and other voracious insects.

The gazebo was huge, like everything Vaughn built, and replete with a small refrigerator, microwave, sound system, plenty of electric outlets for general lighting and for Christmas lights Stevie had strung around banisters and hung from ceiling rafters. It even had its own bathroom and shower.

It wasn't the soothing sounds of the Manasquan ocean, but Stevie loved it, even in winter, keeping warm from two gas fireplaces Vaughn had installed when he had winterized Stevie's private home, as he called it. He understood her need for solitude. As hard as it was for Cassie to leave her world with Brian behind, it was harder for Stevie, whose compass no longer pointed north.

Her childhood and teen years had been difficult. She always missed her father, but she never talked about him. She was too young to grieve when she was four, but she wasn't too young to avoid reality when friends asked if her mom was divorced. No, her dad had died, although she could never say it or explain how or why. She just retreated until she was old enough to confine her dad's death to her subconscious.

Stevie settled into her favorite recliner to finish *Angels and Demons*, and snuggled with her favorite quilts at her side. Even her King's Bluff home and its view of a New York City-lit sky had trouble keeping up with this.

After a few chapters, she relaxed, enjoying nature-sounds and a starry sky, until crunching footfalls intermixed with crickets caught her attention. Someone was coming.

"Stevie?" It was Mason's voice, but why would he be here?

"Mason? What are you doing here?"

He opened the slider. "Came to talk. Patricia and I are leaving soon, but I didn't want to go without saying goodbye." He closed the door, taking a seat next to her. "I doubt we'll see each other before the wedding."

"That long? You haven't even set the date. I'm sure we'll run into each other at some point in the summer, maybe at one of Vaughn's barbeques, where he takes over the grill." She smiled, thinking of Vaughn commanding the grill near the salt-filtered pool while everyone was splashing around.

Stevie pushed up the recliner and waited for Mason to say what he wanted to say, but he said nothing, just gazed around, at the night sky and at her.

"What's going on Mason?" She asked, perplexed.

"Wondering," he paused, began to speak, paused again. Stevie shrugged, indicating she had no idea what he wanted to say and that he should say it. Finally Mason asked, "Did you ever think about us?"

Stevie shook her head, as though she were trying to shake excess water from her hair "Sorry, maybe I didn't hear you correctly. 'Have I ever thought about us?' About you and me? In what way, Mason. I don't want to misunderstand here."

"Us as a couple; you and me, as a couple?"

"Us, as a couple? You're engaged; you're setting a wedding date; I don't fit into your future plans in any way . . . and I never did. From the time I started college, you disappeared. You were finishing dental school and considering dental offers, but the Mason who used to spend hours and nights in Parker's room vanished. So why would you ask me such a question now, after all these years? Are you getting cold feet?" He shook his head. "Having second thoughts?" Again a shake of his head. "Wondering if you've made the right choice?"

That got his attention.

"No," he protested. "Not at all? Why would you say that?"

"You asked the question, you and me as a couple. A man doesn't question his engagement choice unless he's not sure he's made the right one."

"I stopped coming around because you were so young."

"So young for what? When I was younger you almost lived here."

"I'd better go, Stevie. I shouldn't have come in the first place." He stood. "Give me a quick hug before I go."

She threw off her cover and stood. Mason came close to her, held out his arms & embraced her. She returned his hug then pulled away, but he held on and pulled her closer. Pulled her closer and tighter, so she was caught in his grip and felt heat emanating from him. His mouth caressed her hairline, her face, and finally he put his mouth on hers.

Stevie got lost for a moment. Then realizing what he, they, were doing, she pushed away forcefully, stepped back, and slapped his face with all the strength she had.

"You never came around for years; you busied yourself with school, a practice, and hiring an assistant more than ten years younger; you dated, got engaged, and now . . . now? . . . you ask me if I ever thought of you and me as a couple? That's an insult, Mason, and I won't be party to any imaginings you may be having. If you had had any feelings for me, you should have had the courage to tell me after I graduated Princeton, or sooner. Women in college do get engaged, and your Patricia is about my age, maybe younger. So your statement about my being young is bogus. Tell me the truth. Why did you stop coming around?"

She glared at him with fierce eyes.

"Stevie," he stammered, massaging his chin, "I have a dental practice. I couldn't have a wife following news and reporting about the Middle East, speaking out against Israel or Zionism. I have lots of Jewish patients. I'd lose my business."

Stevie was shocked. "As long as I was in lockstep with the accepted narrative, I'd be a good wife?" She turned away. "Mason, I would never do or say anything to hurt my husband or his profession, but my profession, and my personality, make me dig for the truth, & that makes me anathema in your eyes and in society's."

She faced him head on. "But you were part of the class when Rachel's father pushed Samir off the roof. You've seen the devastation one side of the narrative can cause. You've seen the hatred; yet you shy away from the truth. You are not the same gutsy guy who sat in my mother's Shakespeare class, learned about morality, ethics, and saw the destructive quality of hate. Nor are you the same gutsy guy who told me you'd always be there for me. Always, from the time I was ten. Remember that promise?" Her lip began to quiver. "And now you ask me this? How dare you!"

She glared at him with fierce eyes, until the tears came. She could no longer look at him. "Mason, please leave."

Without a word, he walked out.

Stevie let herself cry. Of all the people she had admired, Mason was the one. She had sparred with him over roots and prefixes when she and her mom had moved from Manasquan, and he and Parker had risked terrible weather to bring her to Dr. Harper's condo when her mom had gotten caught in a vicious snowstorm looking for Samir.

But Mason had changed, and there wasn't a thing she could do about it. Some people, maybe most, compromise ethics or morals and take the easy road. Mason was taking the easy road, which excluded her.

But at least she knew why he had stopped coming around. It was better than guessing. She'd move on because she had to.

15

CASSIE'S ADVICE

She was exhausted. She had cried herself to sleep in her gazebo and by Sunday, Easter morning, she was a mess, not physically, forget that, but emotionally.

The recurring scene that had unfolded last night jolted her sense of self and self-worth. Unlike lots of young women she had known or encountered, Stevie was grounded. She didn't stress about boys, dating or not dating, or if she were wearing the latest gloss or mascara, or decorating her nails in the latest fashion; she didn't care about labels, haute couture or which glamour star's sign was ascending and trending. Except for the deep rooted insecurity her father's death had caused, she was realistic and down to earth, and that's why Mason's approach and his kiss had hurt so much.

He had always been someone she felt safe with, safe and protected, and he had always given her reason for her to think that. From the time he and Parker had come after her in that life-threatening storm, he had told her he would always be there for her, but he had said that when she was a kid, not when she had grown into a beautiful young woman who could disarm any guy with a look.

The only person who never realized that was Stevie; so she had never pursued him on that level. But he must have sensed it, since he stopped coming around before Stevie started Princeton. Guess he realized the little girl had grown up and that his fortitude was no match for her charms.

So he took the safe career direction and sought a mate that way. But he should never have transcended the boundaries he had erected. He should have stuck with his commitment and let her live her own life.

His embrace and his kiss made it unquestionable that he had felt a whole lot more for her than he ever indicated, and her kissing him back, until she realized the danger in what they were doing, had unsettled her, like a baby bird lost from its nest.

Next morning, Stevie had sought her mother and explained what Mason had done. Her mom consoled her. "He's conflicted," Cassie said, "and that's no way to start a marriage. It's doubtful he even loves Patricia, not if he held you and kissed you like that, but he's too frightened to take a chance with you. Years to come, he may realize what he's done, but he's hiding now, and the only person who can make him see what he's doing is himself. Forget him, Stevie, or the false hope of what something could have been will stop you from living. Don't let his insecurity become yours."

Mom was right. Stevie had deduced that on her own, but the hurt of it all was still seeping through.

16

JEFF'S CAVEAT

So, Monday, as lively as their morning staff briefings usually were, Stevie could barely manage a smile. She could sense Jeff Bradley was excited about something, but she felt empty. Her cohort who shared her station and copy machines with her must have sensed it because she caught Stevie's attention with a well-placed nudge in her ribs.

"What's wrong, Stevie. This is not the 'you' I or any of us know."

Stevie remained reticent. Lara peered over and looked directly into Stevie's face. "It's a guy. We all know that look; it's definitely a guy. Don't let it get to you. If a guy can make you feel that lousy, he's not worth it."

Lara had a cavalier attitude about life, and her comment, just when Stevie needed uplifting, made her laugh. Good thing too, because right after the briefing, Jeff signaled her to hold back.

Jeff was a kindly man, a bit overweight, but by fifty-six, with a sedentary job, a wife and three kids, overweight was the norm.

"Listen, Stevie, no one's taken a topic from a few weeks ago that I thought you would have jumped at, a follow-up on Israel's embargo of Gaza – what's embargoed, is it legal under international law, how's it affecting the people, that type of story. Then Israel's saber-rattling to invade Lebanon again, which is becoming more probable." He gave her a quizzical look. "Any reason?"

"I wouldn't take Gaza because I don't go along with the accepted narrative. You know that." She hesitated for a second, "and another Lebanon invasion, if it materializes, is too personal for me, but if you'd let me write the story about the embargo the way it should be covered, candidly, I'll take that."

He held up his hand indicating, "pause." Stevie waited. "Stories about the Middle East can become too controversial. We've got Israel, our friend, versus a whole lot of Arab countries that want to wipe it off the map, so I follow the accepted narrative. You can cover the embargo surgically, but I can't let you spew some pro-Palestinian narrative that might get us both fired. You handled the Clean Break article with objectivity and discretion, so I printed it, but a pro-Palestinian slant won't fly."

How to respond, Stevie thought. Be frank. "How can I write the story, when nothing about it is legal under international law, and omit a pro-Palestinian slant? Arabs have been made the villain, the terrorists, by the press because that side works for Israel, and we, the press,

73

perpetuate it. But all we're doing is persecuting an innocent ethnic group.

"Why were the Palestinians victimized after the Holocaust? Why were they the people to lose their land? Why were they massacred by Zionist terrorists when they had nothing to do with Germany's concentration camps? Why hasn't Israel ever been held accountable for any of its transgressions, despite dozens of UN resolutions condemning them for crimes against humanity? Israel wants Palestinian land, all of it, and Zionists have spun the narrative to justify taking it.

"What we do, or don't do hurts them even more because we don't get the true story or its history to the public. Every now and then we address it, watered down, but most of the time, we cater to the narrative, because our papers are Zionist controlled. You believe it but you can't say it. The closest you can come to saying it is that my writing the truth might get us both fired."

She looked at him with sadness. "Read UNGA Resolution 181. It says exactly how the land of Palestine was to be apportioned: a homeland for Jews *in* Palestine, not a homeland for Palestinians in Israel, and even that was unethical, because it was Palestinian land. Zionists want us to believe there was no such place, but there was. Go back to 1603, when Shakespeare wrote *Othello*. Towards the end of the play, Iago's wife says she knew a woman who would've walked barefoot to Palestine for a touch of her lover's nether lip. Palestine, never there? We are so manipulated, controlled – and uneducated.

"But Resolution 181 is important because, even though it did not give Palestinians the right of self-determination, it did give boundaries, and it did give

Palestinian refugees the right of return, and Israel did sign it, although they never intended to keep those terms. If they had, they would have stopped building settlements on Palestinian land, returned it, and allowed refugees back to their homes. But settlements continued, Palestinians remain refugees or behind barbed-wire fences, and we turn a blind eye."

Jeff thought about his young reporter's reply. "Obviously, you know more about this region and its history than I do." He swiveled his chair to face her directly. "Why? Why does the Middle East interest you so much?"

Stevie pondered. "It's the reason I don't want the story about Lebanon. It's personal." She considered telling him, but she had never told anyone. She could not verbalize it, nor was she up for the emotional trauma she'd have to deal with. "Maybe someday, but not now. Do you still want me to cover the Gaza blockade?" Jeff nodded. "And write it as I want?"

"With the caveat, I edit out what I want."

"She nodded. "If you don't edit out too much, I'll do the one on Lebanon, but that one would be slanted. I wouldn't know how to write it any other way. Would that be okay with you?"

Jeffrey nodded. "Same caveat."

"Due early summer?"

"Submit the Gaza blockade week three in May. We'll see if Israel makes a move with Lebanon by summer. Right now, it's who's violating the Blue Line, but if Israel invades, and you still want the story, you can have it."

She nodded. They'd wait till Hezbollah or Israel made a move, but crossing the Blue Line, a division created by the UN, proved Israel's aggression. Data she'd read said that between 2,000 and 2006, the Lebanese had crossed the line less than 100 times, while Israel had violated that barrier at least ten times more. Not much to question there.

"I can cover the groundbreaking ceremony for the Freedom Tower if no one's taken it. Has Lara?"

Jeff shook his head. "She hasn't. You take it. You covered the 9-11 ceremony in 2002. This will be an easy follow-up."

Stevie pondered her next question. What the heck, "For the stories about the embargo and maybe Lebanon, can I travel . . ."

"You asked me that a few weeks ago and I said, 'absolutely not.' Nothing's changed. Reach out to the same contacts, and maybe make the article more human interest. Interview some Palestinians living in the City, and Lebanese if the invasion materializes. They'll give you first-hand information and a feel for what's happening, especially if they have relatives living in the Middle East. Get your facts from wire services for the rest. You are not a foreign correspondent; you are not traveling to the Middle East, ever! Are we clear?"

Stevie turned to go. "Remember, Stevie, no anti-Israel diatribe."

Stevie nodded and left, satisfied. One story about the Mid-East more or less on her terms, maybe a second if Jeff didn't edit out the inhumanity that couldn't be buried forever, and the third, covering the Freedom Tower. She was excited enough to want to tell Wade if he was talking to her; if she wanted to talk to him. There had been no communication since she had left Polly's, and she refused to be the initiator. Nor was there a connection between these assignments and McFadden, so there was no reason to tell him and no reason he would even care.

But two were Middle East, and hopefully, she could write them as she wanted. Maybe she could include a comment in the Freedom Tower story about who made big bucks when the Twin Towers and Building 7 came down and we invaded Afghanistan and Iraq. She'd have to digress from the accepted narrative for those and leave it to Jeff and his red pen to play havoc with the copy. Meanwhile, she had research to do.

By this weekend, she'd make what she hoped would be her final trip to Bradford County. It had been six weeks since her first trip. Wells would be drilled and pumping and Frank and his crew would be moving on to the next site. She'd be able to wrap up her notes, write her fracking story and be done with PA. She'd book her room at Polly's and enjoy a relaxing weekend with two delicious breakfasts. Closure on this story would be over by Sunday.

17

FRANK'S QUESTION

Great day; spring was in the air and she inhaled its fragrance. In a month, she'd be changing her wardrobe to short sleeves and white pants. Another spring, another burst of life, and she just a passenger, watching from the outside as it all went by without her. Her life went from one story to another, and that was it. There had to be more than this. What decisions had she made that had kept her without a husband and kids? What idiosyncrasies or foibles or whatever you called them kept her so alone?

Here she was, walking a construction pad completely up and functioning, being escorted by Frank Goring, a man who had smiled only once, but what a smile. Now that this was her last trip here, it was easier to admit he was damn good looking.

For her, the site needed a mere perusal. Everything she and Wade had seen that had not been completed when they were last here was finished. Three wells, not just one, pumped and purred smoothly. Frank could pull his crew from this site and break ground on another any time so he didn't fall behind with his leases. That was the sensible thing to do.

Since she had come without Wade, Frank had focused his attention on her, knowing this would be her last tour. There was nothing else she needed to see and nothing else he had to show her. He knew she was satisfied, but to be sure, he asked if she had any questions. No, she didn't. She stood still, writing notes, taking in a last look of the wells, and snapped a few more pictures. When she finished, she thanked him for all the time he had given her and turned to leave. She had a great story.

But before she had put one foot in front of the other, Frank surprised her with a question of his own: "Stevie, how about dinner tonight?"

She was completely thrown off guard. Go to dinner with Frank Goring, fracking commander in Bradford County, a man who had dedicated himself to keeping a straight face? He must be joking. Besides, she had come for a story, not a date.

He didn't give her more time to think. "Why not? I don't see Wade with you. If you have plans, I'll retract my offer, but don't misinterpret; I'm looking for a dinner companion, that's all. Things get lonely in an all-male camp." Then with an alluring smile she couldn't imagine he possessed, he caught her by adding, "You know that song from 'South Pacific' about a clean white shirt?"

Stevie burst out laughing, completely disarmed. "'There is nothing like a Dame?' That song?"

Frank nodded. "That's the one, and if you go to dinner with me, I'll have a reason to put on a clean shirt, white or any color. We can talk, eat some good food, and relax. There's a great bar and grill about four miles from here; it serves the best ribs I've ever eaten, and I've eaten ribs all over this country."

"You want me to eat ribs, sloppy ribs dripping with sauce, covering my face, and staining my clothes?"

"Why not? You need to let your hair down and kick up your heels. They even have a country trio that might make you do just that. Wear old clothes; cover them with a pile of napkins. Come on Stevie; have some fun." He waited for her reply, hoping it was yes.

Stevie thought about it. She hadn't really ever let her hair down, as the expression goes. So, she'd get a little sauce on her clothes and her mouth. What the heck; just food, conversation, and a genuinely nice, "careful-with-the-good-looking-part," guy, somewhat austere but who had an alluring smile when he used it, and a sense of humor. "I'll go."

Frank would have let out a hoot if he had been alone, but he replied calmly, "I'll pick you up at 6:00. It gets crowded by 7:00."

Stevie nodded; easy as that.

Frank could barely keep his eyes off her, like the first time he had seen her when she entered the van and saw Wade's strongbox. She was gorgeous, but he couldn't react to it. Most likely, he'd bet, she didn't know it, or didn't make a fuss of it. Her face was chiseled like some Greek goddess; her shape was mesmerizing; her wit could disarm anyone. He didn't know Wade's personal circumstances – they were none of his business, but Frank knew Wade was a fool if he let this one go.

18

RIBS AND BREW

Stevie was waiting in the foyer when Frank picked her up. She wore casual jeans, a long-sleeved, light cotton top, pale gray, with small button studs around a jewel collar. Her hair was pulled back at the sides; the rest cascaded down her back. A few loose tendrils graced the sides of her face, pretty and practical, safe from a rack of ribs. Frank had a feeling Stevie was not the type who would eat ribs with a knife and fork. Gorgeous regardless of what she wore, she had prepared for a possible mess.

With a quick goodbye to Peggy, who, arms crossed, looked Frank up and down, Frank ushered Stevie to his pick-up truck. It wasn't Vaughn's limo or Wade's Mercedes, but it was roomy and more comfortable than she expected, and perfect for his job. She climbed in and they were on their way, talking about her career and his career while listening to country music and Stevie joining in to the refrain of Trisha Yearwood's "She's in Love with the Boy."

Ribs and Brew, a local joint that attracted down-home diners with a penchant for good food and lots of talk, was lit up like a Christmas tree outside and in. Frank boasted he could find the best local restaurants wherever his jobs took him and he sure was right on this one.

Conversation was lively. Several parties of four and one of eight were already seated. Two tables had been served; slabs of ribs were overhanging their oval platters, making Stevie conclude one meal could easily feed two. Three hefty guys were stationed at the bar, downing shots with beer chasers; a few ladies were situated several stools away.

The dining area was huge, but the place was filling up early as Frank had said. He led her to a table for two, off to the far side, halfway between the entrance and a small dance floor in the adjacent room. A three piece pick-up band, banjo, sax, and keyboard, were setting up for an evening of down-home foot stomping.

"Ribs, fries, baked potato okay with you?" Frank asked, not bothering with menus.

Stevie nodded. "With salad."

"I'm sure they can rustle up half a head of lettuce." He signaled to the closest waitress who wove her way between tables to get to them. "Two specials, plus one salad. Oil and vinegar?" He asked Stevie.

"Perfect."

"Plenty of napkins," he added as the waitress, her nametag read, "Sally," turned to leave.

"Special rib platters always come with those," she said. "But you already know that, Frank."

Stevie was not going to let that one go. "A first-name basis? Hmmmm, you do get to know the locals."

"When you're away from home six to eight months at a time, on a regular basis, you get to know locals and local flavor because it reminds you of home."

"Where's that for you, Frank?"

"It used to be Arizona, from kid to high school. University of Texas for undergrad, Cal Polytech for Masters; met my wife there, settled in Texas."

"Both you and your wife went there?"

He nodded. "I may not look it, dressed like this and doing the kind of work I do, but my SAT scores competed with the best."

"I can believe that." She thought about his statement. Just because someone's career involved manual work didn't disqualify him from being highly intelligent and highly educated. She had seen the electronic equipment in the control van from which the entire operation was conducted. You had to be pretty smart to handle that.

"So you settled in Texas and became a fracker."

"No, not right away. For the first few years after we were married, I had a normal 9:00 to 5:00 job, had kids, then I became a fracker."

"Then you left your wife and kids for six to eight months at a time?"

"Yup, left for twelve years . . . and then, she left me.

Stevie tilted her head. "I can understand that." She leaned on her elbows and moved a bit forward. "Did you go after her?"

His turn. He moved closer to her, his face intruding on her half of the table. "I did, but you don't go after someone a fourth time, when the first three didn't change anything. I'm a fracker. She knows that. Only thing she, we, didn't know was that I'd become one a few years *after* we were married."

"Why'd you make that choice?"

He shrugged. "At first it was alluring; the company needed someone who could do an outstanding job and they chose me. So there was some ego, and tons of money, but to be candid, neither of us thought it would become a lifetime career, and when it did, year after year, she wanted a husband, not tons and tons of money, and we parted."

"That's sad."

He nodded. "Yes, it is, but we're friends, good friends. It was an amicable divorce. I saw the kids when I was between assignments. It worked. One lives in New Jersey and works in New York, like you. The other's married; I have a grandchild on the way. What about you? We talked about your career on the way here, but we never got to anything else. Let's get to it now. Home is?"

"Used to be Manasquan. When my mom remarried it became Princeton. After I covered 9-11 from a firefighter's perspective, it became Weehawken, an apartment on Bergenline Avenue, which became a house in King's Bluff, the ritzy area, and the skyline view equals the view from Hamilton Park." She smiled and Frank drank it in."

"Next question: There's no ring on your finger and with your career that keeps you hopping from one story to another, I doubt there ever was."

Stevie became pensive. It was easier to listen to his life than to talk about hers. "There was the thought of someone during my college years; he was my stepbrother's best friend; but he stopped coming around once I started college. He recently got engaged, but not to me." She looked at him with a wan smile.

Frank shook his head. "Whoever he is, you don't want him. Sounds like a coward, runs from commitment to someone he cares about to someone he doesn't. Safer that way."

Stevie looked at him. "You've never met him; know nothing about him, and come to that conclusion?"

Frank nodded as Sally honed in on their table, carrying a tray with two extra-long dishes, each the size of serving platters. Sally barely fit them and dishes overflowing with coleslaw, steaming baked potatoes slit, emitting steam and swimming in butter, a giant straw basket of fries, and a huge bowl of lettuce, radishes, red onion, cubed tomatoes and olives, on their table. Then she squeezed in oil and vinegar cruets.

"That was fast!" Stevie exclaimed.

"Honey, around here we serve these all night and keep the oven going. Can't make 'um fast enough, and they always come out fresh, nothing made yesterday and stored in the fridge for today." She plopped down a pile of napkins more than an inch high. "Enjoy," she said, and left for the kitchen and her next order.

What now, she thought. Frank covered his lap with two napkins, picked up his knife and fork, cut off a wedge of ribs and dug in. Not to be outdone, she followed suit, but added a third napkin as a bib. Frank was right, the ribs were delicious, sweet, juicy, tender, better than she had ever had. "I'd drive up just for this," she said, swallowing her first bite.

Frank smiled. "Good, aren't they?"

She nodded and took another bite. Minutes ticked away as they dove into their potatoes and slaw, gobbling one fry after another, so intent on food that conversation took an intermission. Then Stevie addressed Frank's comment about a guy choosing the girl he didn't love because it was safer than committing to someone he did love.

"So you think the guy I was talking about is a coward?"

"For not going after you? Hell, yes. A woman wants to know a guy cares for her, loves her, and the only way to know that is if he comes after her or is willing to fight for her, take a physical beating if he has to, but she's gotta know he loves her. Then if she rejects him, he gave it all he had. Your stepbrother's friend couldn't or wouldn't do that. Your guy quit as soon as you started college?" Then more to himself than to her, "Probably realized you were a knockout and had trouble dealing with it."

Stevie was taken aback by that comment but didn't pursue it. "He believed my outspoken views on the Middle East would hurt his dental practice."

"They might have. People can't deal with a narrative that goes against the controlling power, but he could have told you instead of running away without saying a word."

Stevie let her fork stab the potato a few times. "When I was young, he told me he'd always be there for me. But he wasn't." She shrugged sadly. "Somewhat of a betrayal."

"Look, Stevie, next birthday, I'll be fifty. I have no intentions of ever misleading a woman or remarrying. But I'm telling you, as a man who's had lots of experience,

87

guys would hit on you all the time if you let them, but my bet is you won't.

"You don't put yourself in places where a guy *could* hit on you. Maybe you were set on this guy so you'd have an excuse *not* to get out and mingle. That's my guess. You work. When you're not working you think about work, and you stay away from anything or anyplace that might get you a guy."

"You don't know me!" She was indignant. How dare he presume to know her insecurities. In defiance, she consumed one fry after another.

"I know the type. Tell me, would you ever have come here by yourself, if I hadn't invited you out?"

"Of course not, why would I? Why would I come to a place like this on my own, or even with a girlfriend?"

He nodded towards the women on the barstool. "They're here, three women, without men. Why not you?"

She shook her head. "That's not me."

"That's exactly my point. Bet if you were here on your own one of those guys would hit on you. Then what would you do? Would you be frightened?"

She thought about his comment. "Yes, I would, but no one would hit on me just because I'm a female or here on my own."

Frank laughed out loud. "Oh you are so naïve. No wonder you don't go out, or maybe it's *because* you don't go out, but a beautiful woman like you? I'm telling you, guys would hit on you all the time, if you were willing . . . if you were out there. Maybe you're no different than your brother's friend, too much of a coward."

"That's an obnoxious thing to say!" She glared at him, "You don't believe me?"

88

"Not at all. It's preposterous."

"Really?" He pulled out his wallet. They had eaten a good chunk of their dinner, fries were all gone, but were nowhere done with ribs. "Work with me on this, okay?"

"Okay what? Work with you on what? What are you doing?"

"Just work with me. I'm trying to prove a point. Sit here, *don't move*," he emphasized. "I'll be back in ten minutes, and I won't be far."

Frank got up, threw his chair back, and shouted so the entire restaurant could hear, "I've had enough of your whining and complaining. Every time we go out, you start in. I'm finished with this." He threw two fifties on the table. "Pay the bill and find your own ride home!"

He walked out, leaving Stevie shocked, stunned, and in awe of what he had just done. She shrunk down into her seat as far as she could. All eyes were watching. They had seen and heard his outburst. How could they not? What would she do now? Fear coursed through her veins. This had never happened to her, ever. She didn't move, not a muscle, not to wipe her mouth, scratch an itch, nothing. Seconds ticked and turned to minutes, and still she sat.

Suddenly, there was movement to her right and the sound of a scraping chair. It was him, one of the big guys, wide and tall, who had been sitting at the bar. He had dragged an empty chair from a table and seated himself diagonally between her and Frank's chair.

Oh my gosh, oh my gosh, oh my gosh. Her hands quivered. "Excuse me, but this place is taken. My date is sitting here."

"I think the whole restaurant saw him leave and heard him tell you to get your own ride home, pretty lady. I can oblige; so can any of the other guys hangin' out at the bar, but I'm the best catch from the lot." His WWF T-shirt stunk and his yellow teeth showed through his lascivious grin. In his mind, he had her trapped.

Breathe, Stevie, breathe; *remain calm. What would other girls do in a situation like this?* Her stomach retched. She was choking; she had to get away; she had to get some air. "I'm okay, really, I'm okay; he'll be back."

"You don't look okay, but you sure are mighty pretty." He reached out and slid his hand across her arm.

Stevie squealed in terror and leapt from her seat. "Don't touch me! Don't touch me!" Her legs trembled. She could barely stand, when suddenly, Frank's steel hands were around the guy's neck, squeezing tightly.

"Don't ever touch her again, you hear me?" Frank emphasized each word with deliberation.

The guy tried to talk, but couldn't. Frank's grip was strangling his vocal chords.

"Something you want to say? An apology, maybe?"

The guy shook his head. Frank loosened his grip.

"You were saying?"

"Lady, Ma'am, I apologize for bothering you. I thought you needed a ride home, that's all. I'm sorry."

Frank released him, and as big and heavy as he was, he spun around and went back to the bar and derisive comments from his drinking buddies.

Stevie felt weak. She was almost crying. "How could you?" She uttered. "How could you do that to me?"

Frank put his arms around her and she leaned against his chest. "If a guy doesn't come after you, or isn't willing to get hurt to defend you, you don't want him; he isn't worth it. This was the being willing to get hurt to defend you part. I can't show you the "isn't willing to come after you" part, but I think you get the message. Your brother's friend? He's not worth it, nor is anybody else who won't. That's what a guy does. It's instinctive, regardless of all the crap your radical feminists want to shove down our throats."

"I hate you," Stevie said, her face still on his chest.

Frank smiled. If he had been fifteen years younger, he would never let her go. But he wasn't younger and he wouldn't ask a woman to live the kind of life he lived.

After Stevie regained her composure. Frank apologized. "That was rough, and maybe I shouldn't have done it, but now that you've been through that hell and have come out fine, do you want me to take you back to Polly's or would you rather stay for dessert and a whirl around the dance floor. That band sounds pretty good." He nodded towards the adjacent room where a few couples were already on the floor.

She thought about it. She could go back to Polly's and cry in her room, or she could shake it off and become part of life. Why not? The masher had been subdued and although Frank's lesson was crude, he was right. She was naïve, very naive. "Let's dance," she said, happy to have the opportunity to move on the dance floor again. "And I will have another beer!" She said with attitude.

"Woah, I've unleashed a tigress." Frank smiled, signaled the waitress for two beers, then ushered Stevie to the dance floor. He hadn't danced in a long a time. This would be a special night. Hell, it already was.

19

BACK TO POLLY'S

What a memorable evening it had been, good wholesome fun - laughter that made her ribs hurt and so much dancing her feet hurt – well worth it. She wondered why she had never gone to a place like this, ever; no home cooked food on the menu in places she and whatever date she was with had gone; no "kick-up-your-heels" band that kept dancers on the floor all night.

Three beers! Did she actually drink three beers? Yup, she sure did, and, for someone who hardly ever drank anything except tea or water, this was like drinking a keg. She was ready to go when she began tripping over her own feet, but the country rhythm the group was playing had become intoxicating. She stayed, she danced, she gyrated, until Frank pulled her off the floor.

"You can't dance like this when there are people around. In your living room, yeah, not here."

She was too tired to protest. When he said, "We leave," she was more than ready to go, crawl into a comfortable bed and not wake up till morning. Tonight she'd say goodbye to two people she'd never see again, Frank and Peggy. She had grown fond of them both but she had her story; there was no reason to come back.

It was past midnight when Frank drove his truck into Polly's lot. It had been a great night for him. If he could get himself to forget her, he'd be fine. He'd double his effort on the next pad, work extra hours, hurry each site and each lease along. By the time Bradford County was done and he was reassigned, her fragrance, her sensuality, would be completely out of his thoughts. But for this one brief night, he was almost young again, almost thinking of aspirations and dreams, almost thinking, and feeling the way he had felt when he had met his wife and dreamed of a future.

But he was close to fifty. Remember that Frank. Remember that and what you told Stevie. He was too old to get serious with a woman at his age, especially Stevie, almost half his age, and ask her to live his lifestyle. She was ready to settle down with a stable guy who could give her a family and be there for them. That wasn't him. He'd walk her to the door, give her a peck on the cheek, and walk out of her life.

"Wait till I get the door for you, Stevie. You might need a hand getting out. Trucks sit higher off the ground than you're used to."

"I got in fine, Frank."

"That was before a hell of an evening and three beers."

He smiled, slammed his door shut, walked around the truck, and opened the door for her. She worked her feet onto the ground and leaned against him. "Come on," he said, putting his arm around her to keep her steady, "I'll walk you to the door."

They were about to climb the stairs when they saw him. "Wade," Stevie uttered, "what are you doing here?"

Wade stood, hands in his pockets, seething. "I came because Peggy told me you were here. Why didn't you tell me you were coming?"

"Excuse me?" She said indignantly. "Why didn't I tell you? I do not need to tell you where I'm going. Why didn't you call? You shut yourself off from the world and me when we were last here, and no communication from you since. There's no reason I can think of why Peggy should have called you to tell you I was here." She glared. "Can you?" He was silent. "So, if you don't mind, I'm with Frank this evening, and I'd prefer you not intrude."

He backed away.

"Excuse me Wade," Frank stated firmly. "I'll walk Stevie to the door and be gone."

He walked Stevie to the door, opened it part way, then handed her his card. "If you ever need someone to talk to who'll give you honest, pragmatic advice, call me." Stevie took the card. "Be happy. Life's too short to be anything but."

Stevie went inside; Frank hustled down the steps on the way to his truck. "I work your property, Wade; that's all, but you might do well to listen to my advice – she's not someone you toy with and not someone you let go."

He hopped into his truck and spun out the drive, leaving Wade to fume and wonder what he could have done better. Everything,

20

WADE REFLECTS ON
TRAGEDY

Except for dinner, Wade stayed in his apartment the rest of the weekend. Not heeding Frank's advice, he did not go after Stevie when Frank had gone; he didn't seek her out at breakfast. He packed his belongings, skipped breakfast, and left Saturday morning, leaving no potential encounter with Stevie.

He didn't know Stevie had left before he had awakened. She had found Peggy in her busy kitchen where her superb foods and desserts came to life, gave her a goodbye hug, and told her she'd come up on her own someday. But like all promises that don't conform to our daily routine, they both knew that, despite good intentions, it was a promise that, most likely would never be kept.

Saturday into Sunday, Wade sat in his apartment, four bedrooms, five all-marbled tiled bathrooms, and reminisced. He stared at his West 52nd street view from floor to ceiling window-walls. Some of the world's tallest buildings rose from the ground floor three levels below.

They could have bought higher, but Debbie had wanted to look from her windows without having her knees quiver. She hated heights, but she loved her view and her three thousand nine hundred square feet of elegant living. She used to joke about that missing one hundred square feet. Where'd it go? Why didn't the architect round up to the nearest thousand? Maybe it was needed for the five-lane pool on the third level? Wade smiled at the memory; tears fell.

This place once blossomed with life and laughter, and the sound of Ryan's pitter patter running through the halls. When she cooked, Debbie would sing along with whatever song was playing. Maid service she loved. Anything that would prevent her from cleaning toilettes and shower stalls she accepted into her life graciously, but she refused help in her kitchen. No one was taking over that role. Wade's continual offers to get her a personal chef fell on deaf ears. She loved chopping and paring and hearing it sizzle in the pan. So Wade joined her, and they became a cooking family, even Ryan, from the time she was two.

All that was gone. No more toys to pick up; no more bathtubs to empty; no more goodnight kisses and hugs . . . just empty now. Emptiness all around him, with the constant reminder of all he once had hanging on walls or in picture frames on dressers that he refused to put away. It hurt. It hurt so much he had decided to put the place up for sale. He had to leave this, the memories, the spectacular nighttime views he and Debbie had shared while sipping wine after Ryan was snuggled in bed.

He had contacted realtors and was about to list when he met Stevie. After one ten-minute encounter with her in Frank's control center, he knew she'd make his situation worse, because he recognized she had the potential to steal the memories he clung to. Even though his tragedy was destroying him, he didn't want to let go. He didn't want to forget his wife and child; all he had lived for. He clung to his memories even more. Would he remember his family without guilt if he chose another? Would he remember them at all?

The worse part of his loss was that he blamed himself. It was a Tuesday morning; the second day Ryan's school had closed so maintenance could put finishing touches on a new heating system. When she looked at him with her big blue eyes with thick light brown lashes, he could deny her nothing.

And on this Tuesday morning, Krispy Kreme donut holes with hot chocolate were on Ryan's breakfast menu. She and her mom would have an atypical sugar breakfast and linger until a few stores opened; then they'd meet him for an early lunch. If he hadn't said yes, if the heating system hadn't needed another day to install, if Ryan hadn't wanted Krispy Kremes from the World Trade Center Mall, they would never have been there. So many roads not taken; so many roads that were.

Then Stevie. He didn't want to meet her. He didn't want to meet anyone. It was to have been a quick in-person encounter with Frank Goring at the fracking site on property he owned. He was supposed to stay Friday into Saturday, talk a bit with Peggy, the only person who knew him well enough to know how much he missed Debbie and Ryan, and leave.

Instead, he was presented with a strongbox bearing a few thousand dollars in U.S. notes and an outspoken in-your-face reporter who turned this find into a search into a past he had never known existed.

What for? Why would a find like this turn up at this point in his life, when he found no reason to live? But something about Stevie motivated him to research and learn a guy named McFadden was his great grandfather and that he had issued a diatribe in Congress about the nefarious Federal Reserve which had most likely gotten him assassinated. What was the purpose of all this, when he had finally decided to sell the apartment and run from that part of his life.

He didn't have answers to any of this, but he realized his behavior had bordered on boorish. That he knew. When he got the courage, he promised himself, again, he'd call and apologize.

21

THOUGHTS OF FRANK

She poured all her energy into her fracking story. All Saturday evening and Sunday she slapped her computer keys, checked and rechecked notes, wrote her introductory straight news paragraph – who, what, when, where, why, and how, stressing the what and how for this story, and once her opener was done, the story flowed.

Most of it she wrote in chronological order and expounded upon each point. First a rugged field that had to be leveled before the construction pad could be laid; next the pad is finished; then trucks filled with water, lubricant and sand roll in; then drilling, vertical before horizontal; then casings poured and the drill bit fracturing the Marcellus Shale. Stevie's story covered it all.

Full description of the vibrant activity on the drilling pad brought the story to life, and she included the daily life of the fracking commander, the crew and the man camp Best Energy had built for them. She smiled, remembering the clean, white shirt reference to "Sound of Music" Frank had joked about when he had asked her to dinner. Actually, she smiled whenever she thought of him. Their dinner at Ribs and Brew had given him a personality, a seductive personality, which, surprisingly, she liked.

Her closing paragraph addressed reclaiming used water from the fracking process. Would the wells hold? If so, for how long? Was danger to a town's water supply inevitable despite supposedly full-proof containment measures? Would the variables of nature present future danger?

These were questions opponents of fracking asked, and they were justified. Once a town's water supply was compromised, money did not trump health.

She printed the story, perused it quickly and gave it a symbolic kiss. It was great. She was sure Jeffrey would agree.

Done with her big assignment, she wasn't stopping now. No rest when you're trying to forget three men, no make that two. Mason was a lost cause. She cut the childhood ties and wished him luck. If he were clouding his real feelings for convenience, he'd need it. When she saw him again, and she knew she would, she'd say hi and walk on.

Second, inscrutable Wade. He seemed like a wonderful person, with all the qualities of a good husband and father, but something was tearing him apart. She wished she knew so she could help, but as she couldn't make Mason's cowardice her problem, she couldn't make Wade's melancholy hers either.

Then Frank, who showed her the most enjoyable and the most insightful evening she had ever had. Once she got over the masher incident, the evening was filled with continual laughter and dancing. Three beers! Never! That wasn't the Stevie she had ever known. So she got a little tipsy, who cared. She had fun, maybe for the first time in her life. Serious Stevie, always reading a book; always studying the dictionary, roots, and prefixes, researching something that had occurred decades or centuries ago, worrying about man's inhumanity to man, finally let her hair down and kicked up her heels. There's got to be more than a serious side to life. There's got to be a lighter side to offset the problems.

And the person who had introduced her to that side had been Frank, with his serious yet easy-going attitude. He was just what she needed . . . but, the problem was, no . . . the problems were . . . first, his age – almost fifty, a twenty-one year difference. He'd tip seventy while she was in her late forty's. Something to think about, especially because she wanted kids. She was sure he'd be a doting father, but how much energy could a seventy-year-old man have when dealing with kids, most likely in their late teens. Second, his occupation. She'd never want her husband to travel from one distant site to another six to eight months at a time. As much as she liked him, it would be a life she wouldn't accept, even though, she conceded, she had felt warm and protected in his arms. *Shake it off; forget him too, especially since he made it quite clear he'd never remarry.* Guess the guy she was destined for was still out there.

"Okay, next project." She said out loud, and began thinking about her Gaza blockade and Freedom Tower stories. She knew she was in trouble when she talked to herself out loud, but knowing Frank would not fit her life and that the only man with that potential had serious issues about something he could not reveal, she needed to keep working. Hell, she'd work on both assignments to forget reality if she had to. Frank was right; Stevie did use work to push away her problems.

She filed her fracking notes in an accordion folder and pulled out the notes she had on Gaza. She'd need more than this. So far, she barely had enough for two paragraphs, and most of that was from past readings. She'd need tons more info plus quotes before this story could exude a personality, which it would get after interviews. No rush on it though. Gaza article wasn't due until late May and the groundbreaking story was due in July. She'd have time for something else before each of these. Be creative.

22

INTERVIEWS & INVITATION

Monday through Thursday, she started interviewing for her Gaza blockade story and thinking about a possible invasion of Lebanon. Doing that story would kill her. But she stayed focused, with a few digressions when she floated between reality and fantasy. Reality was the story she had to write; her fantasies were of Frank who had been encroaching on her thoughts more and more. What would he be like as a husband, a lover, or friend? Her answers were all good. *Stop it Stevie; you're getting way over your head.*

Her Gaza story was sending her into areas of the city populated with residents of Palestinian heritage with first-hand experience of what it was like living in their country under Israel's lock and key. One UN violation after another, which Israel always justified with "We have the right to defend ourselves." *Sure, you have the right to defend yourself on Palestinian land? Keep lying; the press will continue to print it.*

After extensive interviews, she had come away not only with information and great quotes, but with samplers of some of her favorite Arabic foods from several Palestinian-American and Lebanese-American interviews, even though an article about Israel invading Lebanon wouldn't have veracity until an actual attack occurred. But from them, she got the same sorrow Palestinian-Americans expressed, especially when they referred to the former beauty of Beirut, once dubbed the Paris of the Middle East.

On Tuesday, her fracking story hit the second page above the fold. "Fantastic, Stevie. You sure have a knack for hunting out a story. I've already had more positive feedback on it, especially from anti-fracking groups than from anything else in this issue." Jeffrey was effusive with praise.

"That wasn't my intent. I just reported it as it presented itself."

"I understand, but I'm glad it's getting such a good response, whether it's from the protest movement or any other group."

After rereading it, Stevie gave it her own seal of approval; it was great. Then she stuffed a copy into a manila folder, addressed it to Frank Goring, care of Best Energy in Cherry Hill. He was the reason her story was so good, and he deserved to see it. Best Energy would make sure he did.

By Friday, she sat at her desk in a bit of a funk. Her fracking story had taken her through the week on a high, and she had used that high to pound pavement seeking out professionals of Middle Eastern heritage. She had met with two or three a day, but as determined as she was to get thorough interviews from a myriad of contacts, she called it quits yesterday afternoon. She had done one more interview this morning but if she needed anything else, she'd follow up next week. She needed a break from sadness and an extra spark of energy. Today, she was plain tired.

When her phone rang, she sat numb and let Lara answer.

"Stevie, it's the guy who gave you the story about fracking. Should I tell him you're away from your desk?"

Stevie perked up instantly. Frank? Frank Goring? She pressed her incoming call button, "Frank? Is that you?"

"It's me, Stevie," he said with a soft, expressive voice. "You wrote one great story. I'm impressed." The sound of his voice made her stomach jump. "I could have emailed the editor's desk, but I wanted something more personal. It's Friday; I've been thinking about you all week; How about you pick a place low-key like Ribs and Brew, and we celebrate?"

His invitation unnerved her. Her heart was racing, pounding in her chest. He was thinking about her all week? Would this be a date or a continuation of last weekend when they had a fantastic evening and he had candidly said he would never expect anything from her other than good wholesome fun, that he accepted his age and lived a nomadic life?

He read her mind. "I know I told you I was too old for you, much too old, and that I would never hit on you, but I like you and I was hoping we could do it again. What do you think?"

"Not sure. It was easy on your turf when it was a one-time thing, but here? In my world? That's more than a one-time thing. I want a family and stability. I don't want to have to look on a map to show them where their father is."

"Stevie, it's not a marriage proposal; it's an invitation to dinner, maybe a place with dancing, like last week." He didn't tell her that he had thought of much more than dinner and dancing, that he would gladly have offered a marriage proposal and lived with her the rest of his life if he thought she would even consider it. But he knew a yes from her was his own fantasy.

"You're in Bradford County?"

"Uh-huh."

"And you're driving down to Jersey?"

Another uh-huh. "It's only four hours. I'll leave soon."

That would be one long drive, but for a guy who traveled the country, maybe it was insignificant. "There's a small, comfy place about a mile down from Hamilton Park, just off Bergenline Ave. I've been there once, briefly, but when I was there, food and dress were casual and it had a DJ, a small dance floor and an outside deck that offered a panoramic view of the skyline. For a low-key celebration, that's the best I can do."

"I'll pick you up at 6:00, at your house, or if you're not comfortable with that, I can meet you there. Your choice."

Let him close enough so he knows where she lives, or keep distance between them? "How much longer will your fracking projects in Bradford County last?"

He laughed, knowing exactly what she meant. "If it'll end soon, you'll let me pick you up at your house, but if I'll be around longer, you'll play it safe and meet me there?"

"Something like that. It'll be an enjoyable friendship, nothing that'll get me closer to a fifty-year old man who never stays put."

She had him there. "I'll be here at least five more months. I'll meet you at the restaurant."

She gave him the restaurant's name, location, and general directions from the Marginal Highway. He'd figure out the rest.

23

THE OVERLOOK

He was early; she was late. Damn, for a fifty-year-old guy, he sure looked good, too good. His physique could pass for a young man in his late twenties, early thirties, tight muscles, flat abs. A few coarse lines showed near his eyes and mouth, but that was it. Instantly, Stevie sensed danger. He was charismatic, exuded a raw, animalistic charm, and she was not in the safety of a fracking site. Rules having been established or not, she was magnetically drawn to him. Ribs and Brew had broken boundaries a bit, but she had felt safe there. Here she did not. She was glad she had driven her own car.

A replay of last week. Not with ribs, or the masher at the bar, but wonderful and warm, honest conversation. Except for omitting how her father had died, she opened up to him about her life. Between bites of fillet, mashed potatoes, and salad, they talked most of the evening about life in general - where it takes you, phony people you meet, superficial priorities, too much hedonism and id, ego, and a bit of superego.

Frank asked about the strongbox again, something Stevie had almost dismissed. "Anything come of it?"

Stevie shook her head. "Not really. We know McFadden was Wade's great grandfather, that was a shock, and we know he pressed charges against the Federal Reserve's Board of Directors, but not much else. We were supposed to meet to discuss the Fed's tentacles and its control of our government, but he ceased all communication after Gary tied the Fed to wars. Last I saw him was when you dropped me off at Polly's last week."

"Both Gary and I, and a few of my other crew, believe someone other than 'of the people, by the people and for the people' own this country." He paused, put down his fork, and gazed at her, unable to decide whether to say his next thought. Then, with a 'what the heck' attitude, he asked: "You like him?"

That took her by surprise, big time. Stunned that he would even think of that, she had no response. Shaking it off, "Yes . . no . . . ." she replied with hesitation, "why would you ask that?"

He touched her hand. "Because I like you." Then he removed his hand as quickly as if it had touched a flame, "And I don't want you to get yourself hurt because of a story," he said softly.

Warmth surged through her; she blushed and withdrew her hand. It was a beautiful moment, but uncomfortable. Feelings surfaced within her, feelings she didn't want to have. Frank must have sensed it, because he balled his hand into a fist; then picked up his fork and took another bite, as though nothing had happened between them.

Conversation about superficialities resumed; mundane things, like why the need for a new car every year; continual cruises and vacations to distant lands, why a bigger and more expensive house . . . as if three thousand square feet weren't enough.

By the time they had exhausted that topic and were laughing at the direction life takes you, the DJ had switched to rhythm and blues and Stevie was ready to dance. She couldn't believe how easy Frank was to talk to. She had revealed more about herself than she had told anyone; her words flowed. Whatever inhibitions she may have had, had dissolved and it had nothing to do with wine.

Tonight, she didn't need any alcoholic beverage to move to the Commodores' "Nightshift." Frank drank in all her moves, too mesmerized to stop her as he had done at Ribs and Brew. Next song, Marvin Gaye, "Let's Get It On," and without realizing it, she was dancing exotically just for him. Frank watched her steal the show, tangled up in his own feelings. Finally, a slow song, The Righteous Brothers, "Unchained Melody."

"1965? That's my mother's generation," A bit of mischief played in her mind. "Come to think of it," she added coyly, "that's your generation too."

"You can be a real wisea . . ." he caught himself before he finished.

"A wiseass, huh. Is that what you were gonna call me?"

"Yes, I was, because that's what you are." He smiled. Intentionally or unintentionally, she had won him over. He pulled her close; holding her gently. Could this night last forever? They began to sway to the lyrics and music of a love song that had classic status. It was a song for all generations, a song for slow, close dancing that positioned Stevie's cheek close to the sensual fragrance of his aftershave, and she responded instinctively, placing her hands around his neck. He drew her closer. Too late, she realized it had been a dangerous move.

He kissed her softly, a warm, sensual kiss. Rational thought was no longer on the menu and she kissed him back, gently then with passion. She melded into his embrace. All his talk about being fifty, away from home most of the year, never leading her on, all evaporated. Stevie wanted this kiss to last all night. She wanted to be with him as she had never wanted to be with anyone, not Mason, not Wade.

Frank was losing control. The fragrance of her hair, her face, was intoxicating. He pulled her closer, kissing her with raw passion; his desire became intense, until he pulled her so close she became one with his body, and she suddenly recoiled in fear.

"No!" She cried, pulling away from him, breathing heavily. "What am I doing? I'm sorry; so sorry. I should never have done that," she stammered; then broke from him and ran for her purse, leaving him completely disoriented. A second before, this gorgeous creature had been in his arms, making his blood boil. Now he stood there with empty arms, watching her race away. If he let her go now, he might never see her again. She would retreat into her cocoon and reject him completely.

"Stevie, wait. Wait!" He grabbed several bills from his pocket, threw them on the table & motioned their waitress he had paid. Then he raced outside to see Stevie's Buick speeding away.

Faster than he had ever moved, or needed to move at any fracking site, he ran for his truck, started the motor, and followed her trail, desperate, knowing he could never keep up. Her brake lights signaled that she had stopped at the end of the block and turned left. She'd be long gone by the time he got to the intersection.

But he wasn't giving up. He remembered King's Bluff. Where was that? He'd hunt her down, knock on every door, wake up every resident, probably get himself arrested. Who cared; he'd find her. He had to. He had to go after the woman he loved.

24

THE HUNT

He was close. At least he was in the right area, thanks to a bored gas station attendant who would have talked to a statue. He passed every house on every block in King's Bluff. His reasoning told him if she could see the New York skyline from her porch, her house had to be way above the sight-line of the hill. That omitted every house below the incline. Next point of deduction, did she have a garage or would her car be parked on the street? He was looking for a 2002 Buick Rendezvous with a warm engine. Would she have taken the time to raise her garage door, pull in and close the door? Or would she slide into a space on the street?

House after house, block after block, seven, eight miles an hour, slower around corners, and then he saw it, her gray Buick, parked haphazardly in a space outside a brick two-story house; its front porch sweeping the front and sides of the house, bordered by nothing, offering a panoramic view of the New York skyline. Beautiful. No wonder she liked this area. Who wouldn't? Far enough off the main road to avoid traffic, noise, and auto emissions, she could sit out here on her porch swing and watch the beautiful horizon or gaze at the skyline, quietly isolated.

This had to be her house; it was the only corner house encompassing both blocks, with a silver gray Buick half in and half out of the lines. Now his problem. Should he knock, ring, incur her wrath? That couldn't be worse than never seeing her again.

He took the steps slowly, apprehensively. He hadn't felt this way in decades. Four 6 x 6 lights inserted themselves in a strong oak door. He peeked in. Nothing, no light, no sound, no movement. Impulsively, his knuckles rapped the door. Still nothing. He rapped again. A dim light switched on. He backed away from the glass, like a kid afraid to be caught.

She sensed someone's presence. Who was at her door? Who would be brazen enough to knock at this hour? No thief would do that; a thief would gain entry surreptitiously. She put her face to the window, flicked on the porch light; saw him, then flicked it off.

Frank did not try to hide. He faced her directly. "It's me. You know I won't hurt you. Please, Stevie, open the door; let me in."

She shook her head and raised the bat she held in her hand. "Seriously Stevie? A bat?"

Seconds passed. Let him in? And what would happen then? She barely knew him, yet she wanted to be with him for the rest of her life. Did she trust him? Basically, yes, but did she trust herself? Emphatically, no. She had almost initiated that kiss and even now, she wanted to crawl up into his body and nestle there forever. She had loved that kiss; it was soft, sensual, and real. If she couldn't prevent herself from kissing him, if she never wanted to leave his embrace, how much control would she have over her desires if she let him in? But he called to her, a strong pull, insatiable desire she had never felt before.

Inside or outside, she lost. She unlatched the lock and chain and stepped into the night. She couldn't think or utter a word. She just stood there, speechless, leaning against the front door, staring at him. He was almost fifty, he lived cross-country most of the year; he didn't want a wife, stability, or a family. What was she doing here, in her robe, waiting for him to speak?

But he didn't speak. He offered no apology, no excuse, just stared at her, stared with longing, then placed his hands behind her back and drew her to him, slowly, against his chest, against his body, then moved against her, slid his hands along her backside and drew her closer. She gasped, feeling weak, but she could not escape. Her robe opened. He ran his fingers along her breast down to her stomach. Heat engulfed her. When he moved his fingers along her thighs and gently between her legs, she almost collapsed. He held her as she leaned into him, clawing into his shoulders, feeling the urgency to be closer. Reality was gone; he was taking her to another dimension. She had only imagined what lust could be, until now.

Ecstasy. He was inside her, moving in her, bringing her to an intensity she had never experienced. Her nails clawed into his shoulder; her mouth sucked his neck, and her insides exploded. She hit, trembled, hit again, and again.

When she could finally back away, she stood transfixed, mesmerized, tears rolled down her cheeks.

More than anything, she wanted to take his hand, open the door, and lead him inside to her bed.

But she knew what she had done, how weak she had been, and she burst into deep, lugubrious sobs. Pushing her door open, she rushed inside, bolted both locks and slumped to the floor in tears.

25

WADE'S CALL

Vignettes of 9-11 flashed through her dreams like a kaleidoscope whirling bright, multi-colored images in her eyes, mesmerizing, hypnotizing, taking her from one horrific frame to another, and she, Stevie, was immersed in that rubble, belching rubble, regurgitating cinder, ash and soot, claiming three victims she had dedicated herself to saving.

She had lapsed back in time, refusing to get out of bed. She had used these visions as a safety net to hide from the real world and what she had let Frank do. In her whole life, she had never let herself submit to sensual pleasures like this. Someone else had done what she had done last night, and that someone else had loved it, loved it so much she could think of nothing else.

Her ringing phone jarred her back to reality. She stared at caller I.D. Wade Henderson, not Frank, but then, Frank didn't have her number, and why would he call anyway.

He had gotten what he wanted. Why bother with her anymore?

So Wade, of all people, was calling her now, at 9:00 a.m. What could he want? It had been a week since she had walked out of Polly's, the night of her first dinner with Frank. She sniffed back her sorrow, trying to control uncontrollable emotions.

He should have called days ago when she would have been excited to hear from him. If he had, maybe she wouldn't have done what she had done. It didn't matter; it was too late.

She pressed "talk."

"Hi Stevie." His voice was tenuous and weak. "I know you're not pleased it's me; I doubt I'd be if the situation were reversed, but I want to talk to you and apologize for my behavior in person. I've wanted to apologize for our last two encounters at Polly's, but I didn't have the courage. I do now and I hope you let me explain. It's important to me if you'll let me. I'm not saying it'll change how you feel about me, but I believe it would help you understand why I isolated myself from you and left."

The pause between question and answer seemed interminable. Why would his apology mean anything now? Why would it be important for her to hear his explanation? He could have apologized after he walked away from Gary or when he had seen her at Polly's, despite her having been with Frank. Now, he wants to apologize and explain, after she had given herself to Frank? But that was her problem; don't make it his. She'd give him the opportunity, if for nothing else, to satisfy her curiosity and because she certainly had not done everything right.

"Okay, Wade, I'll listen. When, where?"

"It's a little after 9:00. How about I pick you up in a few hours, say 11:30. We can go wherever you want, where you'd feel comfortable, but I'd really like to bring you here, to my place, because what you believe is my bizarre or antisocial behavior emanates here."

She never expected his apartment. She would have felt more comfortable talking in the library or on her park bench in Hamilton Park.

He sensed her reluctance. "It'll only take a few hours at most. I'll send a car to pick you up. I'll meet you at curbside here, we can talk, order something to eat; then a car can take you home. There's no one else in my life I would approach with this; so in a strange way, you are a special person in my life."

No one else? That was a pitiful confession right there. Wade probably needed a shrink more than he needed her, but he was offering an apology and a chance to explain. Why not? "Wherever you want, Wade."

"Here, please. It would clarify everything."

"I'll be standing in front of the monument near Hamilton Park. The car can pick me up there."

"Fair enough, 11:30, monument, Hamilton Park. Tell the driver to give you his name and place of birth – it's Stan, born in Prague, 1964. He's stocky, has blond hair. I use him all the time."

26

CATHARSIS

S tan was punctual. At 11:30, a sleek, black limo pulled up on Bergenline Ave and called her name, "I'm Stan, born in Prague, 1964. I'm Mr. Henderson's private limo driver."

He pulled over as far as he could on the busy street, hopped out and opened the back door for her. Wade had said he'd send a car. She wasn't expecting a limo, but Stan had the right passwords. In less than twenty minutes, he parked under the porte cochere of what looked like a grand, exclusive hotel with Wade waiting at the door.

"Looks like a hotel," Stevie said.

He smiled, shook his head. "They're apartments, high end apartments."

"How high end?"

"Depends what high end means to you."

She really didn't care. This was her stepfather's world, and she and her mother had become accustomed to it, but she'd never live in an apartment building in the heart of New York City. Where were the trees?

Through a spacious and artistically designed foyer, Wade led her to a set of elevators. He pressed "3" but she noted eighteen buttons on the panel.

"Pretty high up," she said.

"Third floor is as high as I go." He stammered at the word, "I." There had to be an explanation there.

The doors opened to a wide palatial hallway, lined with plush carpeting and paintings on the walls.

"This way."

He led her down the hall, opened the double doors to a spacious foyer that led down a short hallway to a spacious living room, maybe forty by sixty, hardwood floors, sleek, modern furniture, window walls and the most spectacular view of the city Stevie had seen on the New York side of the Hudson.

Paintings and portraits decorated the walls, more than a few, but not overdone. Stevie edged up to one in particular she found appealing, a sketch of a beautiful woman, her hair feathering her face, a Mona Lisa smile, and big soft brown eyes, shielded from heavy sunlight by thick lashes. Stevie was drawn to her haunting look.

"Who sat for this portrait?"

"My wife," Wade said softly, with a tremor in his voice.

"Your wife?" Stevie exclaimed. "You're married? Why did you ask me here?" She considered taking her things and leaving.

"Because she's not."

How did he mean that?

"Stevie. I didn't bring you here under false pretenses. She's the reason I can't get it together, the reason I ran from Gary's comment. And that photo on the right wall?" He nodded to a photo of a toddler, an adorable, beautiful little girl with flaxen hair, blue eyes, and a smile that could charm the hardest heart.

Something was wrong here. More was coming. She glanced around the apartment, exquisite furniture, trappings, everything, but if there were a child here, there was no sign of her. Pins and needles coursed through her body. She had a feeling she did not want to hear why this apartment was devoid of wife and child.

"The tragedy affected lots of people, about three thousand, all thinking they'd be home for dinner by 6:00 to see their spouse and kids who were waiting home for them or meeting them somewhere, just another normal day."

He paused and his voice trembled. "But it wasn't another normal day. Three thousand people never saw their families again, and the ones who waited for them, would be waiting for the rest of their lives."

He faced her. "I was one of the ones who waited . . . and will wait for the rest of my life. So you'll have to forgive me if I seem detached and morose at times, because that's how I've been since I learned my wife and daughter had not survived the Twin Towers attack on September 11, 2001. They died on route to the hospital."

His body collapsed into the sofa and he leaned his head in his hands. Stevie's heart melted. She had been there to witness the devastation and death, suffering and sorrow, but she thanked God, she had only been a witness. Wade lost his life there, indirectly, as Stevie's mother had lost hers, as Rachel had lost hers, spouses dead because of hatred and continual wars we had initiated, that had come back to haunt us. And she, losing her father. Had she ever gotten over that? No.

We had destroyed the Middle East, had set it up on an auction block for purchase by a satanic owner who wanted it all, who wanted no opposition as it devoured more and more land from indigenous people, destroyed, devoured and left hopeless, as we ignored their plight and their aggressor's path to total domination. And several of these victims, maybe from despair, maybe for revenge, had brought it to our home so we could suffer as they had. Never mind that the attack and its multi-faceted machinations stunk like rotting meat. Something's rotten in Denmark? Something's rotten here too.

She put her arms around his shoulders and waited as he wept. After a few minutes, he regained control. "I've tried for five years to behave like a normal person, like the person I was when I was young, in college, after college, engaged, married, full of life and vigor." He shook his head. "I can't. I can't get it back. I live in the past; I dream in the past. Not a shred lives in the present or for the future. I'm sorry, Stevie. When I saw you, I thought I could overcome this melancholy." He shook his head. "I can't and never will."

What to say? *Empathize, Stevie. You've gone through this.* "I've seen my mother go through similar tragedy. You only come out of it when life forces you, or you're ready, but no one can make you ready. If I could say one thing that might help, it would be not to give up. Fight it; just keep fighting." She was speaking from her own heart, for both of them.

123

The deep gong of a huge grandfather clock sounded. Half past noon. "Come," he said, rising from the sofa, shaking off his depression, "I'll order lunch, make tea, coffee, both, and we can talk about other things."

He turned towards the kitchen and waited for her to follow. "Oh, before I forget, Frank called a few days ago. He wanted your phone number. Should I give it to him?" There was a look of panic on her face. "Stevie? What happened?"

She couldn't face him; her embarrassment was on overdrive. Frank had contacted Wade for her number? Oh my God. She glanced at him sheepishly. "Did he say why?"

In that instant, Wade knew. "Oh my God, Stevie, you slept with him?"

She shook her head. "It wasn't like that."

"Then how was it, Stevie?" He reacted in anger. "He used his finger instead of his dick?"

She pushed him away "You're disgusting! Disgusting!" She stepped back. "It's not something I've done before, and I'm not proud of it, but you have no right to be judgmental, and vulgar." Her hands went to her hair. "It was my fault. We were on my porch . . . it just happened!" She had beaten herself up more than she deserved, and here she was beating herself up again.

"So you told him where you live, but you wouldn't tell me?" His tone was softer but still angry. He had lashed out from jealousy, unfair and wrong.

"I did *not* tell him where I live. I sent him a copy of the fracking article in appreciation for all his help; he called me at work to thank me. Then he asked me to pick a place like Ribs and Brew so we could celebrate. He met me there. I took my own car, Wade, my own car!" She was in his face.

"We were having a wonderful time, dinner, talking. Then we got up to dance. He kissed me. The bad part began when I kissed him back, and suddenly it became erotic." She shook her head to lose the memories. The images stayed.

"When I realized what I was doing, I left, got in my car and raced home. About an hour later, he rapped on my door." She had calmed a bit. "I didn't know it was him; somehow he found me. I went to the door with a bat. I should have stayed inside. I went out thinking we would talk a few minutes and then he'd leave. It didn't work that way."

He looked at her stone-faced. "On your porch?"

She nodded.

"Standing up?"

"It just happened." She choked back tears. "I need to leave, Wade. I'm sorry. I've messed up my life, your opinion of me, everything."

He took her wrist. "No . . . stay, please. You haven't messed up your life any more than I've messed up mine. You're entitled to a little mess up every now and then. We all are. What happened wasn't the 'you' I'd expect, but it's not so bad. I'm sorry I was crude. That's not me and I apologize. If you can forgive me for what I said, I can be more concerned with your feelings than my surprise." He waited. "Please?"

"Okay," she said softly, drawing her hand across her eyes.

"Besides," he said, changing his tone, "sounds kind of kinky."

"What?!" She went to slap him. He grabbed her hand playfully. "I said that to lighten things up. Aside from my initial reaction being crass, nothing's at all wrong with what you did. Maybe you like him a lot more than you'll admit. Maybe you even love him?"

She considered that. "Maybe I do."

"Come on, smile. It'll pass, one way or the other. This can work itself out. Okay?" He held her shoulders and smiled. She smiled back. "So, let's talk about the papers I have to show you."

"What papers?" She was back in her own persona. "You didn't mention papers on the phone."

"Three reasons for my invitation: One, to apologize for my erratic behavior; two, to explain the reason for my erratic behavior, and three, to show you my research about my great grandfather and the Federal Reserve. I've done the first two; now the third, but we can talk and eat at the same time. You must be starving; I know I am. So, food with notes, and you will find my notes very interesting; they are about McFadden, four presidents and one congressman who opposed the Fed and were assassinated."

"*Four* presidents?"

"Lincoln, McKinley, Garfield, JFK, and my great grandfather."

"I didn't know about McKinley and Garfield." She paused. "Do you still think there's no connection between big money and who owns our country, who owns us?"

He smiled, his first genuine smile. "Oh yeah, there's a connection. Doubt we could prove it though."

Stevie felt comfortable enough to say more than she had when they had been at Polly's. "There's the Fed that controls the country's money supply, and there's Congress and the Executive branch owned by the Fed because our government borrows its money from the Fed.

"Had I known you would be talking about the Federal Reserve and treachery, I would have brought *The Creature from Jekyll Island*, but from memory, that *secret* meeting in 1910, hosted by Senator Nelson Aldrich, who took his private rail car with six other 'money' men, represented one fourth of the entire world's wealth. They met on Jekyll Island off the coast of Georgia. That meeting, so secret they addressed each other by first names only, included representatives for the financial interests of Rothschilds, J.P. Morgan and Rockefeller. It was the basis for the Federal Reserve Act, passed by Congress three years later and signed by their dupe, President Woodrow Wilson. Their objective then is the same as now, global domination and control of the world's money supply. Today they're a lot closer to achieving that."

He nodded. "You've read a lot about this. I'm impressed. I assume there's much more?" She nodded. "Come on," he signaled her to follow, "let's get some food and I'll show you what *I've* found."

He led her into a spacious kitchen with hardwood floors, a huge center island, top of the line white cabinets and appliances. Then he directed her to a seat at an all-white marble-top table, put on an electric kettle and coffee maker, took down mugs, pushed the service button and ordered a platter of shrimp, beef brisket, scallops and fried chicken.

Pages of notes lay on the side of the table. "Let's see if we can organize some raw material for a story. Also I might have found the reason the McFadden side of the family sold their house and property and left the state." He thumped the papers next to her.

"What's the reason?

"They ostracized him; excoriated him. One of the senators from his own state actually said they intended to treat him as though he had died. His own party members. Pretty bad, huh?"

"Party members stick together when it suits their purpose. If they couldn't or didn't want to see the negative effects of the Fed, maybe even then, they were owned by the same cabal that pushed for it, a powerful banking cartel with support from a Rothschild, a cabal strong enough to control a president. Griffin's book ties a secret organization called the Round Table to a network whose purpose was global domination through central banks, war, and government control, regardless of the 'ism' of the country. If that was their goal then, they're close to achieving it."

He sat back, pondering that bit of information. "That's great stuff for an article, or for several."

"Sure it is. I've known some of this for years, thanks to my mother who researched this for her own reasons, but I didn't realize how much power they really had. It's obvious to me now. Remember I told you about the Fed and government control when we first met at Polly's?"

"You did and I didn't believe you. But I do now. So let's organize my notes so you can write a story and include some of what you just found."

"I can write it and include what I mentioned, but I doubt Jeffrey will print it."

"We'll submit it anyway. Jeffrey will do whatever he wants after that."

She stopped him. "We?" She asked, with an, "eat your words" skepticism.

She was referring to their first encounter, the morning she saw the strongbox in Frank's van. Stevie had said "we" would be solving a mystery. His reply had been an emphatic no.

"Yes, 'we.' We'll investigate together, a team."

"What else did you learn about the Federal Reserve and four dead presidents?" Stevie asked.

"Here, there's more." He picked up an attaché' on the opposite counter, plopped it in front of her and took out a file over an inch thick. "I've read almost all of this. Notes on McFadden's speech, other presidents who opposed the Federal Reserve, but I only skimmed the articles about big bankers trying to institute a central bank as far back as Washington." He fanned out the articles like a deck of cards. "Our media reports none of this; nor is it in history books, either. When you were in school, did any text or history teacher say Russia had sent ships to our coastline to defend the Union if Britain or France interfered in our Civil War, because it wasn't in mine."

She shook her head. "Nor mine. I know from my own research, not from textbooks or our media."

"Any thoughts about why textbooks and curricula don't include this?"

"Do you think they would want us to know?" She shook her head. "Nope. What I believe is that the same perpetrators who decide what to print or not to print, media or textbooks, what we hear or don't hear, which country is our enemy and which is our ally, are the same perpetrators who control our money supply and have sent our kids to war for a century. . . ." His look dared her to finish, ". . . and that includes 9-11.

27

DISCUSSION CONTINUES

B y the time the shrimp, scallops and brisket had been gobbled up and only crumbs from fried chicken remained, the table was littered with papers detailing McFadden's speech, assassinations of Lincoln, JFK, McKinley, Garfield, and two attempted assassinations on Andrew Jackson, with his legacy, "I killed the bank!" If they were looking for a connection, it was staring them in the face.

Stevie's comment, "includes 9-11," had unnerved Wade, but he persevered. It was difficult for him, with his military background and five years of service to the country he loved, to believe our government could have known but done nothing to stop 9-11 just to get this country into war. Yet he couldn't shake elements of truth behind it. So much about that attack did not fit; did not make sense; went against laws of physics and thermodynamics; against the government's conclusions, without any explanation for Building 7's collapse. If

Building 7, all reinforced steel, could come down from a fire contained on a few floors, then any building could.

What really unnerved him, though, was hearing her say that Israel had sent five correspondents to cover the attack. He looked at her with consternation as she spoke. "Five dancing Israelis on the New Jersey side of the Hudson, dressed as Arabs, celebrating the attack, were arrested, held over seventy days then released to Israel. During an interview in Israel, one of the five said they had been sent to cover the event. How do you do that? How do you send correspondents to cover a surprise attack of epic proportions when no one, supposedly not even our own government, knew about it?"

He turned away. He couldn't face the contradiction. Most people couldn't. She apologized. "I'm sorry I was so candid, but these big players will stop at nothing to increase their power, getting their New World Order, their world government control, and if that means assassinations, perpetual war in the Mid-East and elsewhere, or a cataclysmic event here, they'll do it."

"Why'd you research all this? There has to be a deeper reason other than your nose for news."

She shrugged; it was her turn to avoid. "My mother did a lot of reading about the Middle East that rejected the main stream narrative. She made me aware the Mid-East has been a primary target of Zionists for over a century, and anyone of significance who thwarted the Zionist plan was 'removed.' Several examples have been imprinted in my mind.

"One of them is Count Folke Bernadotte, chosen to be UN mediator for Palestine, assassinated because Zionist terrorists viewed him as sympathetic to Arabs, even though his mediation efforts for the International Red Cross saved 20,000 people from Nazi concentration camps, including thousands of Jews.

"Another, Alfred Lord Moynes, British Minister of State, was assassinated by Lehi terrorists in front of his home in Cairo. They believed he sympathized with Arabs too. Then James Forrestal, our first Secretary of Defense, committed to fair and unbiased handling of the Palestine question. He opposed basing our decision for an Israeli state on their influence on our country's elections or national security. He was excoriated by Zionist groups and suffered a breakdown. Supposedly in his mental state, he jumped from his hospital room at Bethesda Naval Hospital. New evidence indicates he was pushed.

"JFK may have fallen victim too. He talked about ending the Federal Reserve and insisted Israel give him access to their nuclear plant at Dimona. It took them forever to comply, but JFK's assassination several months before that visit, made it moot. No proof there's a connection, but it worked well for Israel: JFK never ended the Fed and he never saw the Dimona plant.

"Factor in 1967, when Israel attacked the USS Liberty with planes, torpedoes and napalm, leaving 34 US seamen dead and 171 wounded. Our government covered it up, putting a gag order on any survivors. To this day, the real truth has never come to light.

"One final point: in 1946, when Zionist terrorists blew up the King David Hotel in Palestine, they disguised themselves as Arabs. So for me, it's easy to believe Israelis knew about the 9-11 attack and disguised themselves as Arabs to watch the WTC come down from the Jersey side of the Hudson. That attack was good for them, too, because it meant we'd attack another Middle East country." She sifted through his papers. She was certain she had seen it somewhere. "Ah, here it is."

He glanced at the paper she held. "I haven't read that one yet. I printed it because you mentioned it in your article about Operation Clean Break."

She smiled. "Nice. My article made you think." She skimmed the first two pages. "Here it is, about the goal of the PNAC, Project for a New American Century, written a few years before 9-11. I included it in the "Operation Clean Break" article because, if you put two and two together, questioning the attack is logical. Here, PNAC's goal: to promote American global leadership, which is supposed to be good for America and the world. But here's the key: '. . . the process of transformation, even if it brings revolutionary change, is likely to be a long one, *absent some catastrophic and catalyzing event — like a new Pearl Harbor.*' Which takes us to . . . ?"

She put the pages down. Wade looked weary; despair had set in. "Let's quit for today. We can review more another time."

He nodded. "Yeah, I can only do this for so long."

"I understand. You pick the time and place for our next meeting, here again, if this is where you're most comfortable, or my place."

"Here again next week is fine. We've got plenty of room to spread lots of papers."

"Okay." She glanced at her watch. "I'd better be going. I have a few things to do tomorrow before work Monday."

"Me too. By the way, if Frank calls again, do I give him your number? He's tenacious; he's asked Peggy too. You know he's going to try again."

"He called Peggy?" She covered her face and shook her head, "No, don't give him my number. I haven't accepted my indiscretion yet. I won't know what to say until I do."

"Knowing the little I know about Frank, if he can't get your number, he's going to come after you. Knowing the little I know about you; Frank will be seventy by the time you accept your indiscretion."

Two good points. Frank was not a quitter, and she was a prude. "Don't beat yourself up, Stevie. Most women in a situation like yours would be laughing and posting it on the internet. They'd have a field day."

"You're right." His comment lightened her burden. Maybe what she had done wasn't so bad. She was actually happy Frank was trying to get her number.

She collected her things and Wade walked her to the door. "Stan will be at curbside and he'll get you next week too."

"He can drop me off at my home and pick me up there next week." She pulled a card from her purse, scribbled her address, and handed it to him. "In case you need it."

He took her pen, wrote numbers on the edge of her card, ripped it off and handed it to her. "If you need me for any reason, my numbers." He handed her the scrap.

It was a delightful ride home. She gazed at blue sky, white puffy clouds, and buds starting to peek from trees, until the tunnel's black maw sucked them in and the hum of rubber meeting the road lulled her into a fantasy world with Frank, who monopolized her thoughts until they surfaced onto the Helix.

"King's Bluff is up the hill, Stan."

She was home in less than ten minutes. Trust was a good feeling. She trusted Wade, and she hoped she could trust Frank. Warmth permeated her body when she thought of him. Maybe, for the first time, she was in love.

28

THE COIN

A week can pass slowly or it can rush by, daring you to stop it. Same with a day – morning, noon, and suddenly, it's evening. Tie them all together and you have infinity. Stevie didn't think in such metaphysical terms, but she knew another week of her life had flown by and she was with Wade at his luxury apartment in a place glazed over with death emanating from pictures on his walls.

To put her nightmares behind her, Stevie's mom had run from Brian's death, the nucleus of her life. Gazing at emptiness and sorrow on Wade's face and knowing he faced it every second of his life, Stevie now understood why her mother had left. Maybe Wade would have to do the same thing. This place and its stillness was a void preventing him from living, and he was too young to die.

They picked up their research where they had left off last week, only differences being notes she had brought, and lunch. Wade ordered it earlier and he ordered lots more, two shrimp platters instead of one, plus brisket, chicken, scallops, and he added a double order of linguine with white clam sauce. Stevie was in heaven. If anyone could inhale food and not gain an ounce, she could.

A quick review of what they had learned last week and they were into the one, crucial tie connecting 9-11 and Israel. Despite the quote she had read him last week about PNAC's goal, he wanted specific evidence.

"I brought a few papers that show this," she said, passing them to him. "Most people believe Israel was founded because of the Holocaust; it wasn't. Zionists use that to give credence to their theft, but Israel was conceived by Zionists decades earlier at the turn of the century, when they petitioned the Sultan of Turkey to give them Palestine. They asked twice; he refused twice.

"So they went to the British. Even though the McMahon/Hussein correspondence, ten letters, clearly stated that land would be Palestine as it was stated on maps for hundreds of years, Balfour screwed the Arabs and wrote a declaration, a letter which Lord Walter Rothschild presented to the Zionist Organization for approval. They would have preferred it had omitted the sentence that said nothing shall be done which may prejudice the civil and religious rights of existing non-Jewish communities in Palestine, but they got their foot in the door. That was just the beginning."

She rummaged through her notes. "This quote from David Ben Gurion himself, in 1938, shows it. It says '. . . after we become a strong force, as a result of the creation of a state, we shall abolish partition and expand into the whole of Palestine.' All of Palestine was their intent, from decades ago to the present, and the press hides this."

"That shows Zionists always wanted all of Palestine, but how does this prove a connection between Israel and the Fed?" Wade asked.

She passed him another paper with the photo of a coin. "Here's the connection." On one side was stamped the Star of David, on the other, Lord Edmond James de Rothschild, banking magnate. "On the coin it says, 'Father of the Settlement,' and that settlement was Israel. It's an unequivocal connection."

Wade took the paper and studied the coin. He nodded, "Yeah, this is what it says."

"The coin was minted in 1982 to celebrate Israel's 34th anniversary of independence and the Zionists' centennial."

"That proves a tie between Israel and Zionism. It still doesn't prove a connection between Israel and the Fed."

"Rothschilds controlled European banking and were key in creating Israel, financing settlers from Europe, financing the Knesset and in creating the Federal Reserve."

"So your connection is that, since the Rothschilds are inextricably linked to settling Palestine and creating Israel, and since the Federal Reserve is linked to the Rothschilds via Jekyll Island which planned the Federal Reserve takeover of our money, then the Fed is linked to Israel."

She nodded. "If A equals B and C equals B, then A and C must be equal."

Wade laughed. Are you teaching me 7th grade math?"

"No, 6th grade." She smiled. "Factor in everything we've just discussed and it's elementary, my dear Wade. Only thing that keeps the connection between the Fed and Israel quiet while they push ahead with their NWO agenda is character assassination and a complicit press, a very powerful complicit press. After I do more research, I'll tell you how the press was used to sway an American public, dead set against war, to get into it, with the clincher being the sinking of the Lusitania."

He gazed at her with sad eyes. "Stevie, my training was about country, patriotism, America, freedom. Losing my wife and child is killing me, but having to accept that my country, the country I swore to defend and protect, could let this happen for some global domination is undermining the core of my existence."

She placed her hand over his. "This gesture can't be much comfort, but know there's hurt behind it. I can empathize and commiserate. If there's any way I can ever help, let me know.

He nodded. "Thank you. It does help."

"Let's finish with two more papers then wrap it up." She handed him an article that showed two burning buildings, one conflagration surrounding a mere skeleton of a building, still standing. "In the past two years, two buildings burned over fifteen hours, one in Spain, which burned over twenty hours, and another in Venezuela, which burned for seventeen. Neither came down. So why the Twin Towers? WTC 2 burned 56 minutes; WTC 1 for 85 minutes, and WTC 7, the tower that was hit by nothing, came down after six hours. Something's wrong with this report."

"Anything written about temperature?"

"This one. It says, 'The institute's preliminary reports suggest the WTC's supports were probably exposed to fires no hotter than 500 degrees,' so that's *half* the 1,100-degree temperature needed to forge steel, and it's one-sixth the temperature needed to melt steel without fireproofing. So how'd all that reinforced steel come down from a fire that never reached temperatures hot enough to melt it? This whole thing stinks."

Wade nodded. "This has gnawed at me, but...I dismissed it," I had to, to remain sane."

"Lots of people dismiss it, not to remain sane, but because they don't want to believe our country would be complicit in something like this, or would hide the truth from us. But too many questionable aspects of this tragedy imply otherwise."

She passed him other papers she had brought. "Last point, then I quit. Here, eleven days after 9-11, Pennsylvania's governor was appointed head of the Department of Homeland Security in the White House. Pretty quick. The DHS formally opened its doors in November 2002. If our government had known about an impending attack and had stopped it, could they have justified either the DHS or the Patriot Act?"

Wade shook his head. "Americans would never have accepted it, but we were told we were trading freedom for security, and we bought it. Very few would have accepted an act that contravened the Constitution or supported an Iraqi invasion for weapons of mass destruction that were never there, if they hadn't been frightened into it."

"Last point: Iraq is in Operation Clean Break."

She let that connection sink in without saying another word. They had both had enough. They took their wine to the living room. Wade stood at the window, where he had always stood with Debbie, and gazed at the City. It was Debbie's favorite view, her favorite wine, without her. He choked.

Stevie hesitated; then, in a whisper, asked with apprehension, "Wade, what do you want for the rest of your life? Isn't there something that could give you solace or a reason to get up every morning?"

It was as though his heart had stopped, no longer beating, no longer breathing. Finally, he replied in a voice so soft she could barely hear him. "A child. I'd want a child to come home to, to care for, to be responsible for and know she, or he, is mine, for the rest of my life, for posterity. That's what I'd want - a child."

29

NO HAPPY MEDIUM

Another week passed, but she and Wade couldn't meet on the weekend. Business had taken him to North Carolina to finance another golf course. He estimated he could study the schematics, check the layout of the land, site plan, cover a few other items on his list, and be back in a week or two, latest Memorial Day weekend.

That fit Stevie's plans. While she gathered information and collected notes for her Gaza blockade story, Jeffrey had assigned her a story about Mother's Day. "Include some history," he had said.

She had. It hit the papers Mother's Day, perfect, when she was home with her mom.

"Beautiful story, Stevie," Cassie said, I like your inclusion of the day's history. It's heart-warming to know part of its origins served as unification between former Union and Confederate soldiers. Wouldn't it be wonderful to have a peaceful resolution in the Mid-East."

Cassie hugged her daughter. Her not-so-little girl had experienced her own trauma in her life, beginning at a young age. Cassie had never said it, but she hoped Stevie had not erected a wall between herself and men to shield her from the hurt of losing her father.

As Stevie had gotten older, conversations between her and her mom had developed into a deep bond. She could confide in her mother on just about anything, but, aside from Mason's indecent overture Easter weekend, she had never been comfortable confiding in her mom about men. This weekend she did. She told Cassie about Frank and what they had done, his age, and his lifestyle. She held back what she believed prevented her from reaching out to him after she had lost control of her inhibitions.

"Love is love," Cassie had said. "When I met Vaughn, I liked him, then because of the things he did, I hated him, but after I realized his actions had been from love and intense betrayal, seeing his brother fornicating with his wife, that had cut to his core, I understood. But my biggest transition occurred when I realized I had been in denial. I wouldn't let go of Brian because he was your father, and also because I was afraid of accepting another man, simply afraid. Maybe an element of that keeps you afraid of stepping out from behind your wall. I hope you don't let yourself be as frightened as long as I did."

"I've only known him for two months."

"Sometimes you know in two days, or one." Cassie smiled.

"But his age, Mom, doesn't that matter?"

"Only age? Would you marry someone only because he was the same age as you, or five years older, or four, or two? Age can't be the only criterion. Don't use it as a barrier to hide your feelings."

"I understand Mom. I get what you're saying about a wall preventing commitment or judging by one criterion. But twenty-one years? That will matter."

"Of course it will, in time, but would you prefer spending the years you could have with a man you didn't love just because he's younger? Mason perhaps?"

Stevie recoiled. "Where's the happy medium?"

"Sometimes there isn't. It's just what is."

30

DISTURBING INTERVIEWS

S tevie stared at an open folder. A week had passed and she was still ruminating about the conversation she and her mother had had Mother's Day. *Mom was right; I do hold back with men.* Was it because of her father's death? Was she subconsciously afraid to give herself to a man and risk his being taken away? Yes to both. She had to contact Frank. She had to face her fears. Wade had said Frank was still calling. If he had the courage to come after her and face rejection, she had to grow up and do the same, and let life take her where it wanted her to go.

Her mom was right about Frank too. Stevie knew it in her gut. If he loved her, that's all she needed, because she finally acknowledged she loved him. If he did love her, she'd be with him as long as they lived. If he didn't, she'd handle the rejection and move on. She had moved on from Mason; she'd move on from Frank. It would be a lot harder, but she'd have to.

She focused on a file overflowing with several weeks of interviews with people who had family still living in Palestine. She had more than enough material for her story, and more than enough Arabic food in her freezer and fridge: kibbe, hummus, baba ghanoush, fresh from her recent interviews.

She studied her notes, hoping Jeffrey would print this information. Several Palestinian-Americans she had interviewed had thanked her for taking the topic; she promised she would print as much as her editor would allow. She could feel the sadness they felt for loss and destruction of their land. Several had flatly said the UN had no right to give their land to people who claimed ownership by importing settlers who dispossessed the indigenous people.

During one of her interviews, a Palestine-American, educated in France, talked about an international jurist by the name of Cattan, Henry Cattan. In his book, *The Palestine Question*, he had written that Palestine was one of five states formerly belonging to the Turkish Empire that was ready to have provisional independence subject only to being given administrative advice by a Mandatory.

"The fact that Palestine was placed under a mandate did not affect its statehood, or the sovereignty of its people over their country," George Nassar emphasized. "Palestine has always been sovereign. Look it up for yourself; you'll see I'm correct. That's what makes Zionists, and now Israelis, occupiers. They occupy a sovereign state. Usurpation of Palestine's sovereign land has been Zionists' well-planned, long-term strategy, and it's worked."

Stevie pondered George's statement as she left for other interviews. She had never read what he had told her; additional research was needed. She took a break before going to more interviews. Refreshment, even a cup of coffee, had become imperative.

A half hour later she was back to her usual speed, mingling in a Middle East store surrounded by the delicious pastries her mom used to bake when she was young. Pastries, exotic spices, CD's featuring Arabic music. She drank it in; then to more interviews.

Most responses were similar, just additional information in a different form. The unifying thread was how Israel disseminated violence, murder, seizing children from their parents as young as five, for interrogation, and never being held accountable for crimes against humanity.

What was different was the time line and origin of the Gaza blockade. Some disputed 2006 as the year the blockade began. They believed it had begun over a decade before the Hamas victory at the polls this past January. Their first-hand knowledge, or information from families who had never gotten out, believed what we called today's blockade had begun as a gradual, insidious process, almost from the '67 war, when Israel had started to limit exports and commercial production.

Others believed real closure of Gaza began in 1991, when Israel canceled the general exit permit that had allowed Palestinians to move freely throughout Israel and the occupied Palestinian territories.

"Starting in '91, non-Jewish residents of Gaza and the West Bank had to get individual permits to get into Israel," Mahmoud Abbas said, handing Stevie a wedge of kibbe.

"Four years later, in '95, Israel built a fence around the Gaza strip. They penned us in."

"By what right do we allow Israel to blockade us on land that was ours? It is because the great Satan, the US, allows it, since this country is owned by Zionists," Khalil Zaytoon, a corporate lawyer, postulated. In his mind, it would only escalate. "Israel wants all our land. Watch and see. Because of this United States, they'll get it."

Dr. Nassor supported his concern with data. "In the beginning of 2,000, before the second intifada, approximately 18,000 Gazans passed through the Erez crossing every day. Last year, it was fifty. This year, so far, it's zero. Where is the humanity? There is none, only cruelty, subjugating a people who have been subjugated for decades. No one here cares. They read the Zionist owned papers; get the Zionist-slanted news; watch the next football game or wear the latest fashions while Israel ethnically cleanses my people."

He ended the interview there. He could not go on.

That was Friday. She considered another day of interviews, but she had more than enough for her article, and Jeff had given her a week three, May deadline. Here it was, week three.

Her interviews had given her the past, present and future of Israel's illegal occupation from an on-the-ground perspective, and they painted a grim picture of the damage the blockade was causing. She hoped, when she finally got this story together, Jeffrey would print it intact, or at least not cut too much.

Okay, girl, stop thinking and write, write, write, but she couldn't. She had a phone call to make that she had been avoiding for too long. She had to address it before she talked herself out of it again. As nervous as she was, she'd take a break and call. Maybe then she could write.

31

FRANK GETS AN INTERVIEW

"I'll get this motherfucker if it's the last thing I do!" Six men circled their commander, watching him pound a sledge hammer against a coupling that wouldn't budge. Regardless of arms, chest, and a back of rippling muscle, that coupling was not moving. Frank was releasing three weeks of pent up anger and he knew it. So did his men.

He had tried rational thought; that hadn't worked. He had tried working twenty-four hour shifts; that had failed too. Nothing helped. At first, he had taken it out on his crew until Gary told him to fix his own problem without targeting them. His second in command was right. What had happened in King's Bluff at the home of the most beautiful woman he had ever known was his fault, completely. He should be mature enough not to make it someone else's. He mollified his behavior towards his men, but took it out on anything physical that came his way.

Finally realizing steel was stronger than he was, and that his behavior was bordering on insanity, he stopped, threw down the hammer, and inhaled deeply. "Gary, please get some lubricant. You and the men uncouple this pipe. I'm quitting for the day."

That was the first logical thing he had said in three weeks. But how to fix his dilemma? His options were few, since he couldn't get her number from Wade or Peggy. He could call her at work, but she might not take his call. Even if she did, he couldn't tell her what he wanted to say while she was there. His other option was to drive to Weehawken, knock on her door and beg her to listen to his apology.

He'd have to have a damn good back-up plan, though, something that would let her know he was serious. For this he had already taken the first step. He had reached out to Best Energy's Eastern branch office in Cherry Hill for a vice president's position that had become available last month.

At first, he had ignored the posting, but after dinner with Stevie at Ribs and Brew, he considered it. Settle down close to her, a 9:00 to 5:00 job, maybe one or two weeks of travel per year to conflate fracking sites, compare production rates with operations on the ground, make recommendations, and be home fifty weeks of the year. A wonderful life if he had Stevie to come home to. He could not get her out of his mind.

He had submitted his application after their second dinner when he realized he was in love with her; he had barely made the application deadline. He beat himself up for waiting so long until he realized he could never do this kind of work anymore.

He felt like a teenager experiencing first love, and in a way he was. Maybe it was his age, accepting mortality, but he had never felt like this, even when he was engaged. He sat, paced, sat, rung his hands through his hair. The great independent "I need no one" Frank Goring had been skewered.

When his phone rang, he took his time answering. Since it would never be Stevie, who cared who it was. On the fourth ring, he checked caller ID: Best Energy. Woah, get this call. The person on the other end was Matt Hargrove, head of the steering committee for the VP position.

"Your resume is impressive, Frank, and it seems you have a reputation here, a good one, even though most of your work has been in the West. So I'm particularly interested in meeting you in person. I will be heading your interview. We've set you up for this Wednesday, 10:00 a.m. Does that work for you?"

"Wednesday, of course . . . 10:00 a.m. will be perfect."

We're putting you up at a Marriott for two nights, tomorrow and Wednesday. We'll make our decision after your interview. Yours is last.

Yours is last. Should that buoy him or make him feel like he was an afterthought. What the hell. If he didn't get this job, he'd get another. He was finished with fracking. He began packing immediately. He threw his suitcase on the bed, hurled in whatever he thought he'd need, and paused. Why not book himself an extra night and stop in King's Bluff? That would be a bold move. He'd survived on bold all his life, but not for a reason like this. He shook off his uncertainty and called the Marriott. Was his room available tonight? Yes, it was. He'd drive in tonight. She'd be home by then.

32

STEVIE'S CALL

Gary walked in to a man throwing clothes into a suitcase with one hand and holding a phone to his ear with the other.

"What's going on?"

Frank motioned with his free hand for Gary to sit while he continued to talk and riffle through his drawers. He pulled up three pairs of socks and tossed them into his suitcase.

His conversation over, he threw his phone on the bed and exhaled, leaving behind a world of stress. "I fucked up with Stevie. You know and the whole crew must know. They don't know the particulars, but they know something's wrong. My behavior hasn't been exactly normal. " He looked at Gary. "Somehow, some way, I have to fix this."

"You're gonna fix *this*? You fucked up for twenty-five years *before* this, leaving your wife and kids for fracking, and you didn't fix it. Why now?"

"Because this is for the rest of my life. What I screwed up before I can't relive; I can't fix. But this, with Stevie, this I *have* to fix."

Gary reflected on a man he respected who stood before him agonizing and rethinking all his past decisions. Would he come to this juncture in his own life in another ten years?

"Well," he said in a lighter tone, "if you play this right, you could be sleeping with a beautiful woman you love for the rest of your life, or . . . if you fuck up, *again*," he stressed the last word, "you'll be sleeping in a man camp with hundreds of sweaty men." He stared at Frank. "Not a hard choice, is it?"

Frank shook his head. "Not for a second. I chose this life over family once, and I will never do it again. Never, I will fix this. Remember that poster on the bulletin board in the van? Same one in the cafeteria here? VP position at the Eastern branch?" Gary nodded. "I applied three weeks ago. I got a call just before you walked in. My interview is Wednesday with a guy named Hargrove."

"Saw the posting; never heard the name. Sounds perfect for you. You've got more experience and savvy than anyone in or out of this company. They'd be fools not to hire you. Leaving tomorrow?"

"Nope, leaving today and you're in charge. They're putting me up in a hotel tomorrow and Wednesday, but I just booked the room for tonight." He walked around aimlessly. "I need toiletries and a shower."

Gary smiled. "Thinking about a detour? Like Weehawken?"

"Definitely Weehawken. Think she'll see me?"

Gary nodded. "Good plan. Even if she won't, you're making one hell of an effort."

"But do you think she will?"

"Doesn't matter what I think. Besides, you're dealing with a woman. You never know what a woman thinks."

"She would *not* react kindly to that statement."

"Go. Get busy, pack, shower, do whatever you have to do. What I say is irrelevant."

Frank headed for the shower and turned the nozzle on high. After beating up a steel coupling, a hard pulse would relieve some of the tense muscles in his neck and shoulders.

"Want a beer?" Gary shouted. "It'll help you unwind."

"Sounds good," Frank yelled back.

Gary headed into the hallway to the cafeteria as Frank's phone rang. He stuck his head back in the room. "Frank," he shouted. "Frank, you want me to answer that?" The shower was drowning out their voices. He got closer. "Frank, want me to get this call?"

"Get that for me, will you, Gary?" Frank yelled. "Could be the Marriott or Best Energy."

In the few seconds it took Gary to get Frank's phone, the ringing stopped. Gary stared at caller ID. "Frank!" Gary shouted. "I missed it . . . ." He paused. "It was Stevie."

That, Frank heard. He barreled into the room with a towel around his middle, dripping puddles of water in his path. "Stevie? Stevie called and I missed it?!" Frank exploded. He grabbed the phone, stared at the screen; then punched the wall.

"They'll need plaster board to fix that hole." Gary looked at his boss, a stranger now possessed. "Get a grip, Frank. Think of the good side."

"What good side?"

"You have her number."

33

SHE CARES

She had called. She wouldn't have if she hadn't cared at all, and Gary was right - he had her number. The pressure ebbed.

Once Frank had begun to think about Stevie's feelings more than his own, he realized the trauma he had caused her. He knew from the masher incident at Ribs and Brew that she couldn't handle difficult situations with men. What he had put her through that night on her porch had been much worse.

"She'll talk to you, Frank. Stop driving yourself crazy. You may have to persuade her some, beg some, but she'll listen."

Frank nodded. I was going to knock on her door this evening; maybe I shouldn't. Now that I have her number, maybe I should call first." He turned to Gary. "Have you ever seen me unsure?"

Gary laughed. "You? Unsure? Man she has really fucked you up."

Gary left for the cafeteria and returned with two beers. In that time, Frank had showered off residual suds, towel dried his hair and dressed. Cargo pants and an aqua pocket-T-shirt were casual enough. He was ready to go.

They clanked bottles and drank. "I'm no guru with women, Frank, but my gut tells me she's scared. You've told her you're not looking for marriage, not looking to settle down. She doesn't know that's changed. She doesn't know you're in love with her or that you've got this interview and most likely you'll get the job or one like it."

Frank began to pace. "Yeah, even if I don't get this one, my nomadic life is over."

He dug deep in his pocket, pulled out a jewelry case and opened it. A two carat diamond snuggled inside. "This is about as telling as a guy like me knows how to get."

"That'll do, but it might be a bit premature."

"I'll only give it to her if she wants me without it."

"I meant it might be too soon for a proposal."

"Maybe, Frank said with uncertainty, "but if I have to offer it as a last effort to show sincerity, think she'll go for it?"

"Not if you ask like that. You don't give a woman a ring as a last ditch effort and say, "Want to go for it?"

He continued to pace, right, left. "If I knew what she expects from me . . . can't get a handle on that, especially the age difference." He had twenty more good years. Would she take them? "I can fix the other obstacles, but age is age, can't change that. Will she accept a guy my age?"

He stopped pacing, threw a few more things in one suitcase, more underwear, and socks in another, hung trousers and shirts in a garment bag, and zipped them up. He was ready.

"Go. Get your ass to Weehawken. You'll be calmer, regardless of the outcome. Sometimes not knowing is worse than dealing with reality."

"Don't let the crew walk all over you." Frank smiled, hoisting his suitcases. "I'll be back in a few days."

He gave a wistful smile and headed out. The crew would be in good hands with Gary, as good as with him. No problem there. His only problem lay ahead with a beautiful woman who lived in Weehawken, New Jersey, a dynamite reporter who wrote for the *Times*. A classy beauty like her with a troglodyte like him? Getting her would be a miracle.

34

GO HOME

Monday was winding down. Stevie about collapsed in her chair, exhausted. She sat at her desk, hitting computer keys, seeing words flow on the screen in a steady stream as they always had, but nothing coherent, nothing cohesive. Where was the transition?

She had called an old friend from her previous job at the *Tribune* to ask about the Great Depression and its connection to the Fed, but it was nothing more than procrastination to stop her insides from jumping.

Then she had called Frank and he hadn't answered. After five rings, she had gotten cold feet and hung up. What if he didn't call back? She'd shrink back into her shell even deeper.

She shook herself out of her funk. *Write, damn it; write.* If she couldn't push Frank out of her thoughts this story would never get written. One big space in Section A because Stevie couldn't get her mind off a man. She sighed.

Lara looked at her as though a stranger was sharing her station. "What is wrong with you, girl?"

Stevie shrugged indifferently. "Nothin."

"Nothin? That's not nothin; that's trauma. You haven't been the same since your fracking story. Something happen there?" Lara scrutinized and pondered, then surprised Stevie with, "Some of the news crew are going to Ramalla's for a few hours, drinks and appetizers. How about you join us? Looks like you need to get out." Her smile was warm and genuine.

Stevie was stunned. She had never gone with them, not since they had organized their first TGIF on Mondays to start the week. Sort of an OMGIM, "Oh my God, it's Monday," plan which had stuck. But too-serious Stevie had declined then. She had been all about getting the story, as if it mattered.

Lara's smile was infectious. "Lara, that's so kind of you. You have no idea how much I appreciate it. If I can't go tonight, could I have a rain check?"

Lara smiled. "Anytime."

Some invisible barrier between them had broken. She had a friend. She'd definitely join the group another time, a Monday, a Friday, whenever they were going.

She didn't have time to think on it further. Jeffrey had left his office and was circling her desk, checking for any indication of a Gaza story. He sensed something was different with her today. She had seemed tense this morning; now she seemed oblivious to the world.

"You okay kid?" He asked.

Stevie nodded. "I'm fine, Jeffrey, just tired, and all these interviews are kind of depressing."

Jeffrey stopped short and stared. "Go home. Take your story and write it home. You like your park bench. Go sit on that and think. I gave you a week-three deadline; this is it, so go home, this evening and tomorrow too. Enjoy the beautiful skyline. Maybe you'll find your muse. Come back with a story by Wednesday. One day for edits, if and only if you need it, and you shouldn't. Got it?" He emphasized his last sentence.

Or else, is what he didn't say, but what he had offered was a nice gesture. So was Lara's. Both of them noticed she was not herself. Take her story and go home? Why not? It was a beautiful day and spring was everywhere except inside this office. She couldn't think of a better place to be than on her porch or at Hamilton Park.

"Oh, and Stevie, enough of these depressing stories for a while. Lara can't cover the Memorial Day parade. You take it. That should be a break from all this Middle East turmoil. Let it rest for a while.

Maybe a good idea. She did need a more festive environment. "Thanks, Jeff." She nodded, then to Lara. "Everything okay?"

"My parents are celebrating their fortieth anniversary. Can't miss that."

"No you can't. That's a beautiful milestone. Have fun, and congratulate them for me." She packed her notes and laptop and headed for home, a change of clothes, something to eat, drink; then get to her park bench where she could sort out her notes, her story, and her life.

35

HER HAMILTON PARK
REFUGE

Stevie unlocked her door a lot earlier than usual. She threw on a loose pair of light-weight, draw-string pants, grabbed a chicken leg, a wedge of kibbe, an apple, light jacket, laptop and headed up Bergenline Ave to Hamilton Park for what would be a beautiful evening to write. Once the sun began its descent, she'd pack up and head home.

Peaceful. So beautiful and peaceful. This view was spectacular. Given three hours of silence, she could write her first paragraph, give it a good hook, and get the reader engrossed in a chronology of events. Tomorrow she'd interweave her interviews and quotes. That'll give the story flavor and human interest. She'd even include the delicious foods and pastries her hosts had insisted she take.

Why not, inclusion of Arabic cuisine dating back centuries would give the reader an idea of the culture of an ethnic people whose contributions to Western civilization had given them their Renaissance.

She felt motivated. She would show the history of the Gaza blockade, its traumatic effects upon the Palestinians still trapped there, the reactions of Palestinian-Americans living here and their feelings towards the U.S., a country they had once believed would have supported humanitarian rights for them too. But it was not to be, and sadly, her profession was complicit. Maybe if Jeffrey printed her story intact, something positive could come of it.

A stuffy newsroom could never have given her this perspective. She opened her laptop and began to type. She knew exactly what she'd write, and it would be fantastic.

36

DESTINATION HOME

Her laptop clicked in staccato rhythm, her nimble fingers never stopped, barely paused, until the sun began to dip and she sat back to read her draft:

"Two years ago, Israel withdrew troops and settlements from the Gaza Strip to end the occupation. Troops and settlers gone, you'd think that would have helped end hostilities, but it didn't, because removing settlers did not end Israel's control of Gaza's borders, its coastline and airspace, its telecommunications, water, electricity and sewage networks, and its flow of people and goods into and out of the territory.

"So was this an end to occupation? Would this lead to the recognition of Gaza's sovereignty by the US, the UNGA Resolution that announced it or the many UN resolutions that reaffirmed it and censured Israel for its violations? No.

"We're told Hamas is a terrorist organization and Israel has the right to defend itself against terrorists. Then what were Zionists, when they either massacred or dispossessed hundreds of thousands of Palestinians, took their land and imported settlers to usurp their villages and homes? Terrorists all, a fact conveniently ignored, because Palestinians . . . what do they matter? What is a Palestinian anyway? Ignore them and their past. Wipe them off the map; remove them from history books; they never existed. Might makes right and we deal with the mighty, the Zionist contrivance of the promised people going back to the promised land, in defiance of all who live there and the actual wording of the Balfour Declaration.

"So we let Israel shut Gaza's borders; we let them embargo fruits, vegetables, wheat, meat, chicken and fish products, animal feed, hygiene products, clothing and shoes, dry food items, crayons, stationary, soccer balls, musical instruments, and more. But no need to list them all. Become a Palestinian; you'll see for yourself."

She reread everything. Sounds good. Tomorrow she'd interweave quotes and focus on food.

Dusk was creeping in, defying daylight-savings time. She gazed at a majestic pink and purple horizon vying with artificial light from a manmade skyline. Nature was winning; time to go home. She packed up, slung her laptop over her shoulder, wrapped the apple core and chicken bone in plastic and shoved it in her pocket. Good thing she had brought that snack, but she needed more food than that. She was famished.

A brisk power walk down Bergenline and up Kingswood & she was climbing her porch steps, eager to put on loungewear, raid her fridge and relax. Two stairs to go, one stair, ten steps to her door and in went the key. She turned the lock and suddenly froze. Someone was here, on her porch. She dropped everything and screamed. The shadow sitting on her porch swing said, "Sorry Stevie, I didn't mean to frighten you."

37

SHOCK

Her laptop slipped from her shoulder and hit the porch; her notes and folders left her hand and landed in disarray around her feet, a wisp of a breeze curling their corners. Frank left his seat to help.

"Sit!" She screamed in panic. Frank froze." Sit! . . . Sit!" He backed into this seat, afraid to move. Surprising her like this might not have been such a good idea.

Stevie was gulping air. Her heart was racing; her legs were too weak to pull her upright. How did he get here? Why was he here? Hysteria was overtaking her.

"What are you doing here?" She gasped when she regained some control of her voice. "You just show up like this . . . after what happened? What gives you the right?"

"Please, let me talk and I'll explain."

"What's that supposed to mean? I'm not letting you talk?"

This was going to be tougher than he had thought. "Stevie, let me say what I came to say. Then if you want me to leave, I will."

She bent down and collected her papers, pulled her key from the lock, walked to the edge of the porch, and sat, her back against the rail. "Talk."

Now or never, he had to say exactly how he felt. "I came for a few reasons. The first is to apologize for what happened here. If I hadn't been so driven by my own feelings, I would have considered yours first and the trauma it would cause you. I hope you can forgive me."

Stevie could have cried. For over three weeks, she had bottled up feelings of guilt mixed with shame and desire, and his verbalizing it brought the moment to life and slapped her face. Her lip quivered. It was dark with a moon glow diffused by clouds, but she turned away, afraid he'd see the weakness she felt. "Say what you came to say, Frank."

"From the second you walked into the control center; I was mesmerized. You talked about interviewing for your fracking story and poked your nose into Wade's strongbox with such animation I had to leave. You didn't notice because you were in your world and I was in mine. So I kept it professional, until your last visit when you came without Wade and I asked you to dinner at Ribs and Brew. Even then, I kidded myself into believing it was a casual farewell because you'd never come up to Bradford County again."

"And I believed it."

She had responded. He drank that in. "But I was wrong to ask you to dinner the following Friday, because that took it out of separate worlds. That was your world, and it went beyond our professional interactions. That made it personal. A celebration for your outstanding article? I'm sure many, all, of your articles are outstanding, but how many of those contacts who'd given you great stories ask you out to celebrate?"

She couldn't let him take the blame for that. "You had no professional reason to ask. I had no professional reason to go. I should have said no."

He hurt for her. She was wrestling with her conscience. Her cheeks sparkled with residual tears.

"Stevie, I have so much to apologize for, but what I can't apologize for is that I had fallen in love with you. I couldn't accept you leaving my life. I figured if I asked you out on your turf, as you put it, I'd be connected to you in some way.

"That part worked, but I went too far. I should not have followed you when you ran from the restaurant. I should have given you some breathing room and called you a day or two later. None of what happened would have happened, and I would have spared you weeks of turmoil. I am so sorry."

38

WILL YOU MARRY ME?

S he sat stone-faced, silent, taking in every word. Minutes passed. This was her turning point. She either remained afraid and alone for the rest of her life, or she fought her insecurities and expressed her feelings to the man she loved.

"Stevie, please say something. Can you forgive me? Can we start over? I did say I would never remarry and that I didn't want a family, but I take all of that back. I do want that, all of that with you."

She sat, thinking, staring, agonizing over what to say, how to say it.

"Stevie, this is killing me. Say something; tell me to leave; curse at me, just say something."

Her words came in whispers. "I've thought of so many things I've wanted to say to you, about things I should have done in my lifetime but didn't, things I've neglected to tell you from my own personal fear, which you picked up on when we were at Sally's and I denied, but the only thing going through my mind now, that I'm capable of expressing, is you telling me you've fallen in love with me, and I'm afraid to believe it."

"Why? Why afraid? There is no reason why I shouldn't have, as much as I tried to talk myself out of it. But yes, I have fallen in love with you, your kindness, your energy, your passion for what you do, for people and causes, your naivete," he smiled, "and your sexy dancing. Everything I've done for the past three weeks is predicated on you, what you think of me, how you feel towards me, what I can do to have you forgive me. Everything I do is all about you."

She cried, without shame, without guise. At the risk of being ordered to sit again, he went to her and held her. She leaned into his chest.

"Stevie, he said softly," If I change everything you'd reject me for, my job, my nomadic life, would you consider . . ." here's where he'd live or die, ". . . would you marry me?"

The intensity of what he said sunk in. This man would change his way of life to marry her. This man said he was in love with her. He knew her profession; he knew a few of her deepest fears, and he still loved her and wanted to marry her. This man was not Mason or Wade. He was coming after her, regardless of being rejected. Between gulps of air and tears, "You'd change your life to marry me?"

"I would do anything to marry you."

She shook her head. "We've only known each other two months."

"I fell in love with you the second you walked into the van and asked for Frank Goring, but I couldn't believe what I was feeling. Yes, for little more than two months, in that short amount of time, I have been in love with you every moment. Denial only lasts so long. If you love me, there's no reason for you to say no."

"My political beliefs don't follow the accepted narrative; that could get me fired and maybe affect you. I hunt down a story even if it boomerangs. I'm outspoken; I say what I think. That won't bother you?"

"You're you, be you. I'm not your brother's friend who thought more about his career than he thought of you. I'm on my way to Cherry Hill to interview for a job at their Eastern branch. My interview is Wednesday.

"I booked my hotel room a day early so I could see you and apologize; see if I could make it right. If you love me and are willing to take whatever years I have left, that's all I need. Investigate whatever stories you want; write whatever you want, whatever your editor allows. We'll deal with a backlash if it comes. We'll live through it and we'll live where you want."

She looked at him. To speak or not to speak. "You were right when you said I was afraid of commitment, afraid of life; that I ran from men. There's a reason I never faced until you. I let life go by, measuring it from one story to the next, but when you left me to face that masher, I realized how much I'd been living in a bubble, running from commitment.

"I did use my brother's friend as a shield. There's a real fear of giving myself to a man and having him leave or taken away, so I ran from anything that could become a relationship. Calling you was one of the hardest things I've done. When you didn't answer I felt abandoned and frightened; so I hung up. Now you're here, telling me you're in love with me, want to marry me. I can't let fear control my life anymore. My father wouldn't want that."

Her fear stemmed from her father? Frank knew he had died, but he didn't understand why that could frighten her. Someday he would ask, but this was not the time. He held her. "I'll always be here for you, Stevie; I'll always protect you with my life, no matter what." He paused, wondering if she'd think he was crazy. "I'd marry you tomorrow if you'd say yes."

"What?" She looked at him with an 'are you for real?' expression.

"I said I'd marry you tomorrow. I'm not leaving, ever. That should tell you how serious I am."

She was dumbfounded. She had run from love forever and he'd marry her tomorrow. Surprisingly, in her heart, she would, but one thought nagged at her. "You must have said something similar to your wife before you married; yet you divorced after twelve years. How can you promise me you'll always be there for me, when you weren't there for her?"

He'd have to get used to Stevie's probing questions, but he expected nothing less from her. Down deep lay the answer, a reason he had never told his wife, or anyone.

"Okay," he became pensive, "the truth. I was a different person then. I was proud, arrogant, too good looking, and I loved the adoration women bestowed on me. They fawned all over me. When I married Carrie, I loved her as much as I could then, based on love as I knew it. But I didn't love her more than I loved me."

He exhaled deeply. "When I chose fracking, it was an allure, an idyllic illusion and it fed the idea of that strong, macho man. And to be completely honest, although I never cheated on her when we were married, I flirted and led women to believe there was more to come. After our divorce, I followed through, with everyone.

"Only after I played that game too many years, did I realize it was all phony. I'd wake up in the morning next to Tania, or Faith, Ruth Ann, anyone, realizing it didn't matter who it was. It could have been any female and it would have made no difference. That's when I stopped.

"For years, my crew has been my extended family. Maybe that's why I stayed on so long despite it having destroyed my marriage. I had nothing to go home to."

She hurt for him. "That's sad."

He nodded. "Yes, very. When I saw you, I couldn't describe the way I felt; didn't even recognize it; it had been too long. I thought about it as Gary and I walked back to the site. Then I thought about it for days afterwards, but your objective was a story, and then it became Wade. I've never come between a man and his woman; so I let it go and did my job.

"But when you were at the site without him, I got the courage to ask you to dinner. I could deal with a no, but you said yes, and after Ribs and Brew, nothing was the same." His look was intense. "Despite the brief time we were together, you became the focus of my life. Forgive me, Stevie; that's why I called you about your story. I had to be with you again."

He looked downward, rubbed his hands together, through his hair, around his chin. "Now, I want to be with you for the rest of my life, have kids, watch them grow, get involved with sports or whatever they enjoy, if you'll have me."

It was her turn. "I am in love with you," she started apprehensively. This was all new for her. "Not at first sight, but at first smile." A warm glow filled her heart. "Questions like where we'd live, how marriage would affect my job, what changes you'd expect from me, things like that pop into my mind, but they're basically insignificant. What is significant is that I know enough about myself to know if I didn't marry you, a man I love, a man who had the courage to come after me, I'd never marry. I'd be too afraid."

He drew her closer. "So, then, even if it's by default, will you marry me?"

She nodded. "I will."

"Tomorrow, or the next day, or the next?"

"You're serious?"

"Completely serious."

That jolted her, but was it so crazy? She wanted kids, and if she were committing to marrying him and having his children, at his age, waiting to plan a formal wedding would be playing into aging. His logic wasn't irrational at all.

She nodded. "I will. I will marry you as soon as you can get the preacher."

"Well, Ms. Komsky, I think I can make this happen. First, call Sally."

"Sally? Sally from Ribs and Brew?"

"Yup, Sally from Ribs and Brew. Her daughter went off with her boyfriend a few weeks ago and got married by a minister without a marriage license. He's one county over from Bradford and according to Sally, does not want couples to get marriage licenses. Doesn't believe in them; says it's all about government control." He smiled.

"He doesn't trust government?"

"You'd be surprised how many people don't. But that can wait. Calling Sally comes first. After she gives me the information I need, I'll call the minister. We'll drive up when he's available. We could be Mister and Misses Frank Goring by the weekend." He paused to let that play in his head. He'd be married to Stevie, this spitfire who crawled into his heart one morning walking to a strongbox to see what was inside. Who'd a thought.

A cool breeze blew off the Hudson. Stevie shivered despite her jacket. "Go inside; get warm. I'll bring your things in after I make these calls."

She hesitated. "Do you want to stay?"

"If we can marry tomorrow, yes, but I'll sleep on the sofa." He laughed. "One night I can handle; otherwise it would drive me crazy. I can't sleep in the same house with you and not sleep in the same bed. I have the Marriott. But," he said it as though it were an afterthought, "you need one more thing . . . ."

He dug deep into his pocket, got down on one knee, opened the jewelry case and held out the most gorgeous diamond Stevie had ever seen. "Stevie Komsky, will you marry me?"

She gasped. Never in her life had she imagined this, but instantly she blurted out, "Yes, as long as I live, yes." He slipped the ring on her finger. A perfect fit.

39

COMMITMENT

Wednesday. She was back at work, but she was not the same person. Externally she was the same Stevie; internally, someone else had taken her place. Her spirits were light, carefree, euphoric, because, as of yesterday, she was Mrs. Frank Goring.

She and Frank had talked late into Monday night after he had connected with Sally, then the minister. As they talked, she made him tea and warmed up homemade cornbread, spread with butter. To her surprise, it was one of his favorites.

Frank told her the details of Sally's daughter's wedding, the minister's name and phone number, one county over, no marriage license required. According to Sally, this minister believed a marriage license connected the couple to the state. He went so far as to say the license gave the state control over the couple's children. He required witnesses and pictures or videos of the ceremony, signed the entries into the family Bible and gave them a certificate of marriage.

Stevie listened intently and asked a few questions. The minister was available tomorrow morning or Sunday late afternoon. He had a retreat in between. By now, exhaustion was overtaking her, but she heard herself agree to tomorrow, Tuesday morning. They could make it by 11:00, just get up early, shower, dress and hop in the car, like going to work.

When Stevie almost fell asleep at the table, Frank carried her to her room, tucked her in, found a cover and got comfortable on the sofa. He'd see her in the morning, then on to Susquehanna County, marry, come back to Stevie's where they'd have a one night honeymoon. Next morning he'd leave for his interview and she'd leave for work. This would be the last day they would be single.

40

BACK AT WORK

She and Frank married Tuesday morning, followed by an elaborate luncheon in a private room at Polly's. Peggy, Gary, and Frank's special crew were all there to celebrate their soon to be ex-commander's marriage. Gary gave a toast, warning Stevie she'd have to keep a bat nearby to keep this marauder in tow.

Her "I already have one, Gary," caused an uproar. Even Peggy laughed, but Stevie didn't need the bat. Frank knew he had been tamed, and he loved everything about it. The newlyweds returned to King's Bluff that evening and spent the night talking pillow talk and getting to know each other in bed. Stevie wished the night would never end.

But Wednesday morning arrived, and the couple showered and dressed. Frank left for Cherry Hill before 6:00 and Stevie pounded out the rest of her story, interweaving quotes with Arabic foods while intermittently gazing at her engagement ring and the wedding band purchased from the only jewelry store in town a half hour before the ceremony began. It had been a whirlwind they would laugh about when they were older and told their kids.

Smiling, Mrs. Frank Goring walked into Jeffrey's office Wednesday morning and handed him the "final" draft of her Gaza blockade story, the one she hoped he'd print.

"Finished!" She smiled walking in; she smiled going out, and she smiled when he bellowed "Stevie! Get in here now!"

He was fuming, shaking the hard copy in the air. "Did I not tell you . . . ."

"Here, Jeffrey. Since you said no anti-Israel diatribe, you must want this draft."

He glanced at the alternate draft she was handing him which omitted the first few paragraphs and an additional sentence or two. "Are you trying to give me a heart attack, or does making me ill come naturally for you?"

She shrugged, suggesting a hopeless character flaw she couldn't identify. "Neither. I want people to see what we, the press, have suppressed. I want them to know what really happened to the Palestinians; how they had no part in their destiny or the exercise of their sovereignty which they've always had – a fact I've recently learned - and I want people to see how they were terrorized and subjugated through no fault of their own. I want people not only to read a little about what's happening to them, but to feel it, feel the sorrow of a people now occupied by an ethnicity who never wanted the world to forget atrocities perpetrated upon their race, but who have no trouble perpetrating them upon another. That was my intent.

"Since I didn't think you'd print the first draft I handed you, I wrote a second, omitting a few sections, not many or I'd lose important facts, but softer. This one, I hope you accept as is. I left one quote from Ben Gurion that shows Zionists' intention was to take all of Palestine. The article is substantiated with quotes from my interviews, adds a bit about delicious Arabic foods, and explains what's happening today, unless that's no longer acceptable."

Jeffrey stared at his young, brash, very outspoken reporter who had more journalistic aptitude than any young reporter he had ever worked with, but who had more courage and passion than common sense.

"Go on; get out of here; I'll read it. If you don't hear me bellow down the hall, it's a go." Stevie turned to leave. "Stevie, one question. You're part of this young generation. Why do you always hand me your stories in hard copy?" He held up the copy she had given him.

She chuckled. "Old fashioned? No, seriously, I hate reading from a computer and I like the feel of real paper between my fingertips - and I love seeing your red slashes on my copy. Can't do that on a computer."

He smiled. She never held back her thoughts. "Okay, what's next for you after the Memorial Day parade."

"Fathers' Day, June 18. That'll be good, and I'm thinking about a topic you might find 'iffy.' It's a peaceful Palestinian movement that began last year, called BDS, for boycott, divest, and sanction. Of course that would be against Israel, and they're labeling it anti-Semitism, but it's worthy of mention."

He shook his head. "What else?"

"After the Father's Day story and the Memorial Day parade Monday, I'm covering the Freedom Tower groundbreaking in July, and perhaps an invasion of Lebanon if it occurs.

"If you want something else, I was thinking about the Weehawken Waterfront, harmless, or the Federal Reserve, not so harmless. When I was in Bradford County, the fracking commander," she said nothing about husband, "and his crew dug up a strongbox with the initials WPH on it. It contained several thousand dollars in U.S. Treasury notes, not Federal Reserve notes. Somewhere there might be a tie to JFK and perhaps his assassination."

"Any proof?" Stevie shook her head. "Then leave it. And even if you did have proof, leave it."

"Don't you ever question the Warren Commission Report?"

His eyes bore into hers. "Stevie, I'm not stupid. Of course I do, but people who have dug too deep wind up dead."

"Okay . . . then what about a story on the history of the Federal Reserve without the intrigue?"

He looked directly into her eyes. "We will not discuss this further. My advice to you is never write a story about this."

Although his answer was disappointing, it was reality. Simply let it be. She'd tell Wade. Whatever research they did after this would be from curiosity, not for publication.

"Keep me posted on anything else your nose ferrets out, and be careful Monday. Leave early. It gets crowded and parking's hell."

"Will do."

This time when she walked out of his office, she couldn't imagine why he'd call after her again, but he did.

"Stevie Komsky!' His bellow could be heard everywhere. "What's that on your left hand?"

When she walked into his office this time, her smile radiated from ear to ear. She held up her left hand and the diamond sparkled on his desk, walls, and the ceiling. "You're married?" His shout reverberated into the hallways.

Suddenly, her cohorts spilled from offices, the copy room, the coffee cubby and hallways, converging on her amidst echoes of chatter and exclamations, all looking at the rings on her third finger, left hand. The ladies surrounded her with a cacophony of who, what, when, and showered her with hugs and kisses. For the most part, it was a female thing, something every woman understood instinctively. Lara gave her a kiss and nodded, understanding Stevie's mood swings since she had come back from Bradford County.

For the men, the single men, this beauty was off the market.

41

LOTS TO CELEBRATE

Six-thirty a.m. Monday morning, no earlier than her usual workday, Stevie was Brooklyn bound. It took less than five minutes to reach JFK Boulevard, first leg to the Eastern Parkway and the parade. Hard to believe a Jersey girl had never crossed the Holland tunnel before, but provincial Stevie never had. So she was giving herself ample time. You never know, with her terrible sense of direction, which she had inherited from her mother, she could get lost easily. And then there was always "survival-of-the-fittest" parking Jeffrey and the news room warned her about – get there early, find a parking space, sit in your car and wait.

She was prepared, overly prepared, with food, drink, and Holland Tunnel history, just in case. Just in case what? What other person who uses the Holland Tunnel researches its history? And why? But that was Stevie, with an open laptop late Sunday morning and a husband trying to get her back in bed.

Frank had come back from Cherry Hill Thursday. He had driven to her house day after his interview knowing she wasn't expecting him. He surprised her not only with his arrival, but with a roasted chicken and mashed potatoes. He could cook!

Jeffrey had given her Friday off as a wedding present for having to give up her Memorial Day holiday and the couple enjoyed every minute. Another wedding present was the phone call from Best Energy saying Frank had gotten the VP position.

They had lots to celebrate and an extra day to do it. They spent the weekend riding the Spirit of NJ and strolling around the City; they had dinner at a posh restaurant on the Weehawken waterfront; took walks to her park bench, spent time in the rustic and very charming library, and to cement a memory, spent an evening of dinner and dancing at the Overlook, where Stevie had first kissed Frank and run out.

She stored each memory in her mental scrapbook, living in a fantasy world until she got up Sunday morning to research the Holland tunnel, directions, and a bit of history for her Memorial Day story. That was a step back to reality.

"Did you know over six million ceramic tiles were used for the tunnel walls, that it cost forty-eight million, four hundred thousand dollars to construct, and that fourteen men died during construction?"

Frank didn't know those facts, but he knew the tunnel was completed in 1927 and that forty-two fans blew clean air in from the floor, and another forty two blew dirty air out through the ceiling.

"And," Stevie continued, reading from the screen, the tunnel is 8,500 feet long, over a mile and a half."

"Not interested," he said, lifting her off her chair and carrying her back to bed.

As for directions to Brooklyn, she had enough to get her to the Manhattan Bridge. No more interruptions from her honeymoon weekend. If she needed directions after the Manhattan Bridge, she'd ask a policeman.

42

RELIVING HER DAD'S DEATH

Her trip was going better than expected. Surprisingly, traffic on Route 9S and 139 was light, but it was early and it was a holiday. People would sleep late. She would have loved that, but she had the parade to cover and Frank had gone back to Bradford County Sunday evening to pack the rest of his things.

Now that his fracking life was officially behind him, and he was Best Energy's new VP in charge of conflating all production and expenditures, he was collecting what he'd left and saying goodbye to Gary and the crew. He'd been with them so long. Tomorrow, he'd drive from Bradford County to the two-week rental Best Energy had given him while he hunted for an apartment or condo.

So Monday morning, there was no reason for Stevie to stay in bed. She was up, showered, dressed, and whizzing through the tunnel in no time. The trip from Canal Street to the Manhattan Bridge had a few stalls, but other than that, nothing. From there, it was a direct line from Flatbush Avenue. She didn't even have to look for a police officer; she knew the way.

Now where to park? With row after row, street after street of parked cars, this was going to be a problem. But she had been warned. Up and down one block then another, the same blocks, same streets, twice, three times, she crawled, looking for a coveted space. She was prepared for a heavy walking day, but she didn't want the walk to begin too far from the parade site.

And then, after what seemed an eternity . . . that car was pulling out! A miracle! Two spaces up, a car had started its motor. The driver tapped his brakes and signaled to his left. Yes, he was leaving. Great. It was a good, roomy space and closer to the main drag than she had expected. Although parallel parking had never been her forte, she backed right in. Perfect. No one was getting this spot.

She sat for a while, organized her thoughts, almost pinched herself to make sure she was in the real world and married, married to a guy she absolutely adored. Then she grabbed her backpack, hoisted it over her shoulders and started for the reviewing stand where all entries passed and all dignitaries sat, ready to give introductory speeches and tribute for fallen men and women of all wars.

Suddenly she stopped, mid-stride, realizing the reason for this day's celebration. It was sad, and it hit home. It had been an assignment she had taken to help Lara. Working on a holiday didn't matter. Journalists work when the story is happening. But for Stevie, who had gotten so caught up with Frank, inner turmoil, and being married, she hadn't remembered the significance of this parade and that it was a memorial for all servicemen who had never come home. That meant her dad.

Her feet went no further. She had to come to terms with this and quickly. Seeing floats, drummers and marching bands, local unions, borough presidents she'd have to interview, and maybe even the mayor, with all their revelry, pay tribute to a memory that included her father, was something she had to confront before she stepped into its midst. This parade and what it represented was a tribute for her dad!

Why had she never thought of this before? Maybe because she had never been to a Memorial Day parade. Never. Her mother had never gone, most likely to avoid something that would sharpen a cruel memory. She understood what Memorial Day meant from the time she was a kid, and yes, she knew this parade was a tribute to the fallen, but since she had never gone to one, where spectators were waving red, white and blue flags and clapping as floats rolled by, she had never felt its aura. She had been to the Macy's Thanksgiving Day parade several times for a joyous reason; for her, this reason was anything but.

Her mind raced back twenty-three years. She was a four-year-old child again clinging to her mother who fell to the floor after those men in uniform told her that her dad had been killed. Just as quickly, her memory shifted and she was on her dad's shoulders, surf spraying in her face, in her hair as little Stevie squealed with delight, oblivious to the specter of death behind us, or ahead.

When you're a child surrounded by innocence, 'dead' is an abstract, a four letter word you just hear; you just say. You never understand it until you're older and all that remains is an 8x10 picture on your dresser that you finally hide in your drawer to make the hurt go away.

Shake it off, Stevie. Shake it off. You have a story to cover.

She made it, despite her trepidation. Eastern Parkway, punctuated with grass, benches, trees, and areas for placing a chair where you wanted to sit. Various speakers were already on the dais. Although she had never met him, the Grand Marshall had to be the man standing close to the mic. Top military brass were in uniform, two women wearing name tags too small to read from where she stood were talking and checking lists, and a minister identifiable by his collar would be giving the invocation. A few others whose roles she couldn't identify milled around; one seemed vaguely familiar.

She was about to get closer and introduce herself when she heard her name. Wade was hailing her from a distance, and approaching quickly. He seemed happy and casual in his demeanor and in his dress too, wearing a horizontal striped yellow, beige, and white golf shirt and beige slacks, more informal than usual, except at the fracking sight when he dressed in work boots and jeans.

"You made it! When you called yesterday to say you'd be back for the parade, I never expected you'd drive through the night."

"I did." He gave her a big hug. "I used to march in this parade when I was at the Point. When you said you had to cover it, I wanted to be here."

He stepped back. "Now, Mrs. Goring, before we do another thing, let me see that beautiful ring Peggy told me about." She held out her hand; Wade took it, looked at her left finger, then at her. "He made a great choice, Stevie, and not just with the ring." She beamed. "I wish the two of you every happiness.

"Now let's watch this parade, so I can reminisce about being fifteen years younger, while you can get me caught up with what's happened in your two weeks. Then I'll tell you about mine. You will be surprised."

They found a perfect viewing spot and talked until the parade began. Once it did, floats that represented Vietnam Vets and several American Legion chapters rolled by. Girl Scout and Boy Scout packs marched. Interspersed between the floats, high school bands, two outstanding drum corps, and three pipe bands with their eerie wail, marched. "Taps," "As the Caissons Go Rolling Along," and "God Bless America," were played in succession, in unsettling tones.

As the participants marched, parade organizers and the commander of Fort Hamilton spoke. The chaplain gave his invocation, and the Grand Marshall encouraged spectators to remember all those who had fallen, remember them not just today, but every day, because they sacrificed their lives and their futures so we would have ours. Stevie felt a certain satisfaction that her father's ghost walked with these marchers. He was still with her; he always would be.

She and Wade marched along for the last part of the parade; then they found empty space on a bench and sat. "I should have shown you this before the parade started, but we were so busy talking about your wedding, I waited till our attention could focus on this." Wade pulled a thick but narrow brown leather-bound notebook, about 5x8 from his back pocket. "Take a look," he said, handing it to her.

194

She took it tentatively. "Wade, this looks old." She opened it and flipped through worn, faded pages and words written in script. "This is *very* old, and the words have been written in ink – liquid, inkwell ink." She looked at him.

"They were. Stevie, this is one of my great grandfather's notebooks." She looked at him non-plussed. "I told you I had something to show you. This is it."

"But how . . . ?"

"How'd I get it? Not easily; I searched every phone book I could get my hands on, searched online and, thanks to you, went to the historic society in every major town I stayed in or passed through. That's why I was gone so long.

"Finally, in a town called Leland, I found the McFadden name. Once I had an address, I followed through and located a distant cousin who owns half the land in town. We talked for hours, two days. He corroborated everything we had learned about Mc Fadden, our great grandfather, and he believed everything you and I had talked about. Only difference is that he has the McFadden name. He tries awfully hard to stay under the radar."

Stevie looked puzzled. "How?"

"He keeps a low profile, uses cash, not credit cards, for almost everything he purchases, even the land – bought most of it from neighbors in cash deals a little at a time, as did his father and grandfather before him. They want nothing to do with the government. The family even got married using ministers who refused state marriage licenses.

"That's exactly what Frank and I did! Sally's daughter and her boyfriend did that; they went to a minister who rejected marriage licenses – said licenses put the government in the mix, that people never needed state licenses to marry until the early 1920's. The couple and witnesses would record the marriage in the Bible and the minister would sign a certificate of marriage."

Wade nodded. "I know; Peggy told me. She told me you married without a license in a church in Susquehanna. Wish I could have been there. But until this past Friday, I was still meeting with my cousin and conflating all the research you and I had done with seven decades of history. I'd like to show you several specific pages from this journal, if you don't mind, if we've covered all the details of your wedding."

She nodded. "We have, and what I didn't tell you, I'm sure Peggy did." She smiled, knowing Peggy had most likely talked to Wade several times from the minute Stevie had asked her to be her witness.

"Yeah, she did." He smiled almost bashfully. She even told me things you ignored, like what was on the menu, what your wedding cake looked like and how Frank put the old fashioned "Just married" sign on the back of his truck."

"Yeah, he really did that," Stevie said, laughing.

"Okay, so let me show you some of these pages." He turned to a few bookmarked pages. "Here, read these two, and then," he flipped to another bookmark, "these in the back, near the end."

43

REMINDER OF 9-11

S he was so engrossed in the handwritten words of Louis T. McFadden dating back over seventy years that she never heard the Grand Master's speech, encouraging spectators to visit the crosses and flags at the Park. Her focus was on McFadden's denunciation of the Federal Reserve and its financing foreign countries, a global agenda back then. Even in the 1930's, McFadden was intuitive enough and smart enough to realize the Fed's objective was to make themselves wealthier than they already were. It had nothing to do with preventing boom and bust cycles.

"Wade, this is a find. Not only is this journal priceless because of its age and provenance, but because of its content. Imagine if his message had gotten out to average citizens and they had listened? He could easily have been killed to prevent that."

"Agreed, but you have to read more, and this is not the place or time. How's this weekend or the next?"

"Let me see which is better for Frank."

"Aha! Your freedom has been curtailed already."

"Hmph." She gave him a defiant look. "Not curtailed. A shared life includes courtesy. Let me see if he wants to do something. He's searching for a condo around Cherry Hill. Maybe he'll want me to search with him or look at something he's found."

"We could make it the weekend after." He pulled out a wallet-sized calendar. "That would be Saturday, the seventeenth, or after."

"Wait, the eighteenth is Father's Day. Can't do it that weekend; we'll be staying at my parents."

Wade dipped his head and became pensive. Too late, Stevie realized what she had said. "Wade. I'm so sorry. I should never have said that." She had to be more aware that celebrations or events common to her were no longer part of Wade's life.

He shook it off. "June 18 will be Father's Day whether you say it or not. It's not something you would have thought to avoid." He brightened. "Whatever's better for you and your *husband*." He emphasized Stevie's new marital status. "There's no rush. We can even wait till the 25th."

The parade was breaking up. "Wade, give me a few minutes. The parade's over and I've gotta catch some of these dignitaries before they leave. Come with me if you're not in a hurry. See how I make my living." Then she whispered, "Sometimes getting a story is not a pretty sight."

198

She climbed two steps on the risers, heading for the Grand Marshall, Wade behind her. With her press credentials in full view, she asked salient questions about the history of Brooklyn's parade. She had already researched its origins, but she wanted more personal data, like organizational difficulties, donors who made it possible, how it grew since 1867, quotes, things like that.

After she interviewed the Grand Marshall, she read the tags on the women's shirts that were too small to be read from afar when she had first arrived. Key organizers of the parade, they gave her information she could definitely use. She followed up with the man who looked familiar. Wade lingered behind and struck up a conversation with the ladies. They were easy to talk to and today, so was he.

This man was the borough president. As they spoke, Stevie suddenly remembered why he looked familiar. His hair had grayed some; lines inserted themselves deeper on his cheeks and around his mouth, but she recognized him from five years ago; he was the man who had defended her when she had donned the fireman's gear and had gotten recruited to help pull people from a collapsed building. After a minute of questions and answers, he remembered her too, realizing where he had seen her.

"You. You are that crazy young reporter wearing a firefighter's uniform who was about to get in lots of trouble for helping rescue those people buried under a ton of rubble." He shook his head repeatedly. "Gutsiest thing I've ever seen a reporter do. Gutsy and noble."

"Don't know about either of those attributes. I just knew I had to give it everything I had to help save them. If it had been me, I would have hoped someone would have done the same."

"Well, young . . ." he stared at her credentials . . . "Ms. Komsky, you did a remarkable job. We should have had you speak here today. That last line you wrote was a tear-jerker. I've never read a news story quite as moving."

He answered her questions and they said their goodbyes. She was left to think back to that unforgettable nightmare and the little she had done to contribute.

"What story, Stevie?" Wade asked, behind her. She was unaware he had been listening.

He drew her out of her reverie. "Oh, nothing, just a story I had gotten about 9-11. Horrible. What I witnessed was horrible, but that man, he's the borough president of Brooklyn, he had been there. Saw the whole thing and got me out of a tough time with officials when I was trying to help. Strange how people remember things, and how they crop up years later, completely unexpectedly."

"He said that last line was a tear-jerker. What'd you write?"

She shook it off. "Too sad to talk about; it took a long time to sublimate. I don't want to resurrect it, ever."

"Okay," he said, changing the subject, "call me when you know which weekend and we'll go over this journal."

"Okay, but we'll be doing this for ourselves. Jeffrey won't print any dissection about the Fed. So when we meet doesn't matter."

"Understood." He could hope Jeffrey would relent, but Stevie's statement was emphatic. "We'll finish up with whatever new information you've gotten and with my great grandfather's journal."

"New information I've gotten is about sinking the Lusitania. I mentioned it when I showed you the coin minted with a Rothschild and the Star of David, but I found a quote from the Congressional record in 1917 that'll show you the role the press played to sway an American public into being sympathetic towards war. I'll show it to you when we meet, plus lots more.

"Sounds good, so would the weekend after Father's Day be good?"

"That's Sunday, the 25th." She nodded. "I'll see what Frank prefers and I'll bring the last research I intend to do." She smiled, hugged him, and they parted, Stevie to her car, and Wade most likely to Stan who would be waiting for him somewhere close with his limo, a nice easy ride home.

44

ODDS & ENDS

Stevie alternated between hitting her computer keys and reading her notes. She had everything she needed to wrap up her Memorial Day story, just a few more paragraphs, a closing and she'd be handing it to Jeffrey tomorrow.

Frank had called twice; once to tell her he was at the rental apartment, and another, late in the night, to tell her he missed her so much he'd drive up to be with her until morning. Not a good idea, since it was already 11:30. She'd be exhausted tomorrow and so would he. Any other weekday, she'd love it.

Tuesday morning, a bright sky and sunlight were streaming through her windows. Although she was still tired, she refused to stay in bed and let the morning go by. She was up and out earlier than usual, but as expected, Jeffrey was already behind his desk. She nodded hello and submitted her story. He took it, gave it a quick perusal, and grunted an okay.

It must have met his satisfaction because he didn't summon her back to his office with his usual booming, "Stevie, get in here!" But a story about a parade was innocuous. Aside from inserting one line about the tragedy of sending our soldiers off to foreign countries to wars we should not have been in, it was a feel-good tribute to all those who had served and sacrificed.

What next? Her Gaza story would be in print today. She hoped her Palestinian-American interviewees liked it. Her next idea, BDS, had been nixed. Jeff wouldn't accept a one-sided article against Israel and she didn't have the energy for the fight it would need. She considered other story lines between now and Father's Day, but other than the Weehawken waterfront, which Jeff was considering, nothing. She'd start Father's Day. Whatever came next would have to fall in her lap. She opened her laptop as Lara came in. "How was your parents' anniversary celebration?"

And that began a conversation that lasted longer than they had ever talked. Lara thanked Stevie profusely for covering the parade so she could be with her parents. "Never hesitate to ask me when it's something as important as that," Stevie replied.

Lara smiled. Stevie was happy to have helped, and it had worked out well for her too because she had gotten to see Wade and his great grandfather's journal. What a find. She had also interviewed some nice people.

By the time the workday ended, she was impatient to talk to Frank. She had begun to feel incomplete without him, and she called him as soon as she got home. They talked while she ate a Cuban sandwich from her favorite deli on Bergenline Ave.

They talked into late evening about Jeffrey nixing the Federal Reserve story, she and Wade continuing research despite that, and his condo hunting.

"Any luck?"

"Two possibilities. One's a community in Ramblewood, a little west of Best Energy, and the other's a three-bedroom condo in Bordentown Township, about twenty miles from Princeton. If you want that one, it would be a short trip to see your mom when we stay here on weekends."

Stevie liked that. She could spend quality time with her family, and Frank could get to know Vaughn better. Actually he would be meeting everyone for the first time Father's Day. They talked about his job starting Monday. Stevie wondered how Frank would adjust to an office setting when he had worked in nature for decades. It was a new life for them both.

"So which weekend would you prefer I meet with Wade?"

"After Father's Day so you can come down this weekend or next and check out these condos. Whichever one you pick; we'll still have to furniture shop. None of them come furnished, and I wouldn't want that anyway. Don't think you would either."

"Not – at - all."

"So how about you meet Wade on Sunday the 25th. I'll drive here when you leave for his place, and we'll have Saturday for ourselves. Think of something you'd like to do."

"One thing," she said flirtatiously, "and you already know what that is."

"On that subject, we think alike, but on another, why do you want to continue your research when Jeff's clearly stated he won't print it?"

"Because so many people have no idea big money, government spending, and a cabal that profits from war affects them. We work, pay taxes and our government never accounts for what it spends. They print more money, increase the debt ceiling, and keep on spending. Doesn't matter if the candidate is an R or a D, they spout a different platform but they're both controlled by the same power behind them."

"Honey, I love you for your tenacity, but you can't influence the powerbrokers of the world."

"Maybe when we have a couple of kids and I'm busy changing diapers, some other tenacious reporter will pick up the baton. After the kids are grown, I'll be too old."

"No, you won't. You'll pick it up again and fight so our kids will have a safer life."

She thought about it. Frank knew her better than she knew herself.

45

FATE DIRECTS YOUR LIFE

S tevie's Gaza story ran in Tuesday's a.m. edition; her Memorial Day story ran in the afternoon. Wednesday her phone never stopped ringing. Five calls from Palestinian-Americans she had interviewed thanking her for a sensitive, accurate piece on their plight, and a call from Brooklyn's borough president, James Farley. "Call me Jim," he said.

He was holding a fundraiser Thursday evening and wanted Stevie to cover it. "Yes, there'll be other reporters there. A fundraiser is a magnate for the press. Even if they hate your guts, they'll be there to get info to hang you. But I'd like you to cover it as well. You have a flair for words."

Of course she'd be there. Thursday evening. She'd write the story in the evening and finish it Friday in work. Jeffrey liked the idea and, even more, he liked the fact that a borough president had personally requested her.

Friday morning, she was writing a review of Jim Farley's fundraiser. Factor out the speeches, most were a bit winded, and she had actually enjoyed the evening. Dinner was good; the company was interesting; conversation lively, and her host, Jim, removed himself from politicking to talk to her one on one, give her insights about his campaign and aspirations for his borough. The evening had gone well.

She printed her hard copy and walked it to Jeff by afternoon, then sat back and exhaled. Lara was extemporizing about a first date she had had with a guy she had met at her parents' anniversary celebration. "He's a friend of my brother's and he asked me out for dinner last night."

So far so good, but Lara had just begun. "Stevie, he was on his phone all night, through drinks, dinner, dessert, and he couldn't pat himself on the back often enough. Good riddance. I would love to date a guy who's interested in someone other than himself, if only for an evening."

Stevie thought about Frank. Their dating had been minimal, but during the few dates they did have, they had talked about everything, even character flaws. He had talked about his family and his mistakes, and had asked about hers. He didn't notice she had not mentioned her dad, but aside from that, there wasn't a thing she felt she couldn't say.

The topic about her dad would come eventually. She was coming out of her shell, out from behind her wall. It was becoming easier for her to think about her father and know his death had nothing to do with the man she married leaving her or being taken away. Gradually, Stevie was leaving her nightmares behind.

After talking with Lara, Stevie realized how blessed she was. Funny how fate directs your life. She wouldn't be married to Frank had it not been for that night on her porch. She never would have faced her deep insecurity and had the courage to say yes. But he was true to his character; he had come after her when no other man had. Warmth coursed through her body. She gave a silent hoot and thanked God for everything, even something as simple as never being in the dating scene again.

46

JIM FARLEY

Her next story did fall right into her lap. Monday, mid-morning, June 5, Frank's first day at his new job and Stevie gets a phone call from Jim Farley. Would she accompany him to a blighted area of his borough to visit a neighborhood slated for gentrification? He was requesting funding from the town council and the mayor, and a story about the area might sway their decision in his favor. Of course she would cover the story. Jeffrey's smile said he approved.

Jim arrived in his own car and introduced himself to Jeffrey before he took his young reporter into Brooklyn to survey the apartment complex in question. Raze it and rebuild two-story garden apartment-style units that provided residents with sunlight and the ability to walk out their front door and be outside. He'd put a picnic area in the back.

Stevie took notes and photos of the area. Jim's plans would gentrify the area, but she asked about cost to the taxpayer and if these new apartments would fall under rent control. Her questions surprised him, as though he didn't expect her to concern herself with the dollars and cents intricacies of his proposal.

"You can't expect residents to support this proposal if they don't see how it's going to give them something back."

"Fair question. This project will benefit the entire area by increasing property values; contiguous areas do have lots of individual homeowners. We'll drive around before I take you back, and I'll send you dollars and cents facts later in the week."

"Sounds good." That would be good groundwork. Then she thought about groundwork for another story. "I'll be covering the cornerstone ceremony July 4th. I assume you'll be there?"

"Of course I'll be there. In fact, I'll be inspecting the preparations for the ceremony next week. Want to come along and see for yourself?"

"Absolutely."

"I figured you would. No one with a nose for news like yours would want to miss an invitation to that."

47

WEEHAWKEN'S
WATERFRONT

Two days later, Stevie received Farley's financial proposal for his gentrification project. Writing while reading her notes and using piano fingers to fly over the keys, she got the story to press for Thursday's edition. Aside from a caveat here or there, it had a positive slant. Farley was pleased.

She followed that with the article about Weehawken's waterfront. She had estimated two, maybe three days for research, interviews, and writing, ready for print by Tuesday, maybe Wednesday of next week. Nope, a huge miscalculation.

By Wednesday of next week, she had not finished her interviews. Research had taken longer and officials were busy, busy with meetings, jobs, and emergencies. Getting back to her with a time and date took her into the following Monday, but by then, she had plenty of information. All she needed were supporting quotes.

She had learned the ferry system had been completed along the waterfront in 1987, and that an eight minute ride across the Hudson provided enjoyable transportation from Port Imperial in Jersey to West 39th Street for thousands of commuters.

She had also learned a three tiered system tied a fine-tuned schedule of New York busses designated 'Ferry,' to take passengers to the terminal, while on the Jersey side of the Hudson, the addition of NJ Transit's Light Rail system made the ferry accessible by rail, bus and car. Eventual cost for the terminal and Light Rail had been approximately twenty-five million. In her opinion, that was well worth it for what it provided.

After she met officials, political representatives, and New Jersey's governor, she had plenty of info and several outstanding quotes. They had all concurred that this project had advanced New Jersey's future growth in commuter trips across the Hudson River.

As she put the story together, she concluded that the whole of the Waterfront transit system had been more than a sound investment. The story was ready for print Thursday, and 100% positive, perhaps the main reason it had been so easy to write. Father's Day story next.

48

MEET THE FAMILY

Perfect timing. Her Father's Day story was in print today, when Frank was meeting her mother, Vaughn, and her whole family for the first time.

They loved her story, but they loved Frank more. Instead of Vaughn being the center of attention, today it was Frank. Cassie's hugs and Vaughn's pats on the back were a little overwhelming for him, but they drew him in. For a man who had distanced himself from family far too long, they absorbed him into theirs immediately.

Julia, in her inimitable fashion, could not control her flippant, outspoken manner and gushed over her sister's husband, pulling Stevie aside to ask if he had a younger brother. Finally, impatient with her young sister who had been brought up to have more manners than she ever displayed, Stevie told her to shut up and behave.

But Frank enjoyed every minute with his new in-laws and found Julia's antics amusing. For him, a man who had lived with a man crew for decades, the weekend was more than he had expected. He talked football with Vaughn, Travis and Samir; kicked around the soccer ball with Sonny; talked with Cassie at length and caught a glimpse of the tragedy the family unit must have experienced when Cassie mentioned her first husband had been killed. "Killed." Stevie had never used that word.

Parker and Rachel, with Hillary's help, were devoting their time to their new baby girl, giving them little opportunity to mingle, but Frank was ecstatic being around a baby again. And Vaughn, his billionaire status obvious, never showed or flaunted it. He was the kind of man Frank respected.

On their way back to Weehawken, Frank expressed his admiration for them before Stevie had said a word, but his accolades triggered a non-stop monologue about her mother, step-dad and brother, about Hillary, Rachel and Samir and a bit about his history. She loved her younger brother and chatty sister, who rarely controlled her mouth. Stevie talked the entire trip from Princeton to Weehawken, more than she had ever talked, probably more than Julia had talked all day. In fact, Frank had little opportunity to interject more than a succinct comment or a grunt of approval now and then.

Frank admired the importance Stevie placed on her family. Too many kids today give a cursory thought about their parents. Frank was glad Stevie didn't fit that paradigm. As soon as they were off the main highway, he put his arm around her, drew her close and gave her a suffocating kiss.

"You are amazing and so is your family. I couldn't be happier." He gazed at her with love. "I don't want or need

214

anything else in my life for the rest of it, as long or short as it will be."

Stevie snuggled close, pondering the vagaries of life, thinking how she had gone to Bradford County for a story about fracking, and had come back with an amazing husband who completed her life."

49

MEETING WITH WADE

The week flew by and another Friday rolled in. Frank had come home early so he could shower her with flowers and dark chocolates which Stevie loved, to celebrate their one-month wedding anniversary. She could rewind that entire week and remember every sentence that had passed between them.

His early arrival completely surprised her. He hugged her as soon as he walked in, told her he was the happiest man alive; then swooped her in his arms and carried her upstairs. Around midnight, he lay supine on the bed, full of passion and desire, but exhausted from the week and the drive. "Time to rest." He turned to Stevie for a response. Surprisingly, she was asleep.

Saturday, a repeat of Friday evening interspersed with food shopping, cooking a gourmet meal, and buying living room furniture for their condo. Sunday arrived too soon. She was almost sorry she had agreed to meet Wade. She was losing interest in a topic that would never see print, but Frank encouraged her. "Research until you're satisfied the note in Wade's strongbox can't take you any further." He was right. She would research for herself, not for print.

Stan was picking her up at 12:30 instead of the usual 11:30, which gave her an extra hour to enjoy a leisurely breakfast, rummage through her desk, and sift through notes she wanted to show Wade. By 12:00, she was ready, they both were. Good thing too because Stan was early. His limo pulled into her drive, motor on idle, while Stevie was shoving papers into her satchel. She kissed Frank goodbye, hurried out and hopped into Stan's limo. Frank left a few minutes later.

As usual, Stan dropped her off at the apartment building's classy entrance. She made her way to the third floor where Wade was waiting at his door. He welcomed her with a hug and ushered her into his spacious kitchen and the same delicious buffet he had ordered twice before. Despite having eaten a full breakfast less than three hours ago, she only needed one invitation to dig in.

She was excited to see him. Even though they knew Jeff would never print anything about the Federal Reserve, Stevie had brought her research from *The Creature from Jekyll Island,* plus other research relevant to their 'Who Controls Us' objective.

As they ate, Stevie mentioned the groundbreaking ceremony she'd be covering July 4th. "Want to go?"

"Would love to," he said. "I've been to most of the memorial ceremonies. I'd like to be there for this."

It made perfect sense he'd want to be where the cornerstone memorial to all those who had perished on 9-11 was being laid. "I'll tell Jim. 9-11 is what the ceremony is for.

For the next hour, they involved themselves in small talk and a bit about the gold standard and fiat currency. Wade complimented her on her articles about Father's Day and the three-tiered transportation system on Weehawken's waterfront, but he especially liked her article about Israel's Gaza blockade.

"Good writing, Stevie. You make any topic interesting because you draw the reader in. I can see how your interviews with Frank, your story, and you, of course, captivated him." He looked directly at her. "If I didn't have an incubus around my neck, I would have gone after you myself."

"There'll be someone for you, but the incubus has to fall off first. You're young. You need to live life. Debbie would have wanted that for you. Don't you see?"

He did. All he needed was a jolt to become part of life again. But neither of them had any idea what it would be. "Something will present itself, in time."

50

A COMPLICATED MESS

S tevie wiped her hands clean of fried chicken before holding McFadden's journal. She turned pages very slowly. "Amazing find, Wade. Don't ever let this go." After several minutes, she passed it back to him.

In the months since she and Wade had first seen the strongbox in Frank's van, she had read a limitless amount about the Federal Reserve and the previous two centuries. Yet, despite her reading, she admitted she had little to no understanding of the true interplay of money. She understood the game with fractional reserves and assets, but the effects the Bank of North America, the First and Second Banks of the United States, Lincoln's three National Banking Acts, the Federal Reserve Act, Bretton Woods and the gold exchange standard had on economics, told her she knew nothing about finance and the monetary system.

"I can read it on paper, spout a few facts about what our government did to create a fiat paper money system, but liquidity, assets, debt, easing or tightening the money supply to determine interest rates, dollar devaluation, international trade . . ." She rolled her hand to designate a whole lot more, then she rolled her eyes, "those concepts make my head spin."

"Stevie, the vast majority of people have never even heard about the things you've just mentioned. No way they'd understand how our money system works. My minor was business and I don't fully understand it."

"Maybe that's the intent. Maybe big banking gurus want it to be confusing so the average person has no clue and they block it out."

Wade shrugged. "Good point, because what people like Andrew Jackson and my great grandfather denounced has become our way of life. No one questions it today. Ever talk about this to colleagues or friends?"

She nodded. "Yes, but infrequently."

"What kind of reaction did you get?"

"They believed the Fed is as American as apple pie and income taxes, and that it keeps our economy running smoothly."

"Exactly. So you shouldn't be surprised that you don't understand it. At least you know it exists, and that detractors have been assassinated over it, even though we can't prove it. You know a lot more than most people who think the Fed rescues the economy when a blip occurs, without realizing banking cartels may have caused that blip when what they allowed got out of hand, or, when they wanted that blip intentionally."

"Thanks, for the confidence boost. Basically I put my faith in two of our Founding Fathers who opposed central banking. Thomas Jefferson was one. He saw it as an instrument to favor business. He also claimed the Constitution gave Congress, not an independent, private, banking entity, the authority to regulate weights and measures and issue coined money. The second was James Madison. He believed Congress hadn't been given the power to incorporate a bank; so powers not given to Congress were retained by the states. My gut feeling sides with them."

"I'd go with that. Power corrupts. So does money, two primary reasons for assassinations and war. Governments are not exempt. If you want to control the world, do it by controlling the world's money supply. Didn't a Rothschild say something like that?"

"You've been reading about the Rothschilds? Now you sound like Gary." She smiled remembering the brief exchange they had had when they were in Bradford County, when Wade had walked away. "Did you read that Lincoln's Secretary of the Treasury, Salmon Chase, was a Rothschild agent? Perhaps he influenced Lincoln to pass his National Banking Acts."

Wade sat up. "Another Rothschild tie."

"They crop up in many places. Although Jeffrey won't print any of this, and we'll never know what your grandfather had intended when he buried that strongbox, I'm not sorry we began this. I learned so much. In fact, I learned more than I ever thought I didn't know, if that makes sense."

"You probably know more about presidents, the politics behind them, beginning with our Founding Fathers, and the Federal Reserve, than freshmen or sophomore college students. That's impressive. It's as if you had gone back to college."

She rolled her eyes again. "I studied enough in college; I'm waiting for the fun part of life. I do find the Fed interesting, though, because it affects everyone's life, past and present. When the country was on a gold standard, you could take a $20.00 bill to the bank and you'd get a $20.00 gold piece in return. I can't even comprehend that today, but that standard did not allow for today's fractional reserve banking. Would we have today's global economy if banks couldn't loan 90% of a depositor's money? Doubt it. Bigger is not always better, but that's me talking; global bankers would disagree.

"Griffin's book also gives insight into dissention between Andrew Jackson's administration and Nicholas Biddle, his director of the Second Bank of the United States. You need to read about that, because it shows the power of money and how our Congressmen were bought by banking powers more than a hundred fifty years ago. How 'bought' do you think Congress is today, after almost one hundred years of a central government bank and several huge lobbies which donate generously to their campaigns?

"Lincoln did sign banking acts that smacked of central banking, but he also believed if we were going to have fiat money, we should have the government print it rather than borrow it from a bank and pay interest. We would save billions. One article I read said his intentions were to nullify the banking acts he had passed."

"And there, Stevie, may lie the reason he was assassinated. *Bankers* wouldn't make billions. Billions of profit and government control seem like the perfect reason people who opposed the Federal Reserve died."

"Who owns us? Andrew Jackson said the Fed was a den of vipers and he would rout them out. He was talking about the Second Bank of the United States sucking the lifeblood from our country. Same with your great grandfather's speech."

"My great grandfather's speech got him dead. I am convinced of that and I believe this same cabal caused the death of my wife and child. I never accepted it before I met you; now, it's constantly in my mind." He stabbed at a few shrimp still on his plate. His fork hit harder until he threw it down in frustration. He had drifted back to things in his personal life he couldn't fix.

"Remember that old song, "I owe my soul to the company store?" Stevie smiled, attempting to lighten Wade's spirits, remembering how Frank had disarmed her when he had referenced a song from *South Pacific*.

She succeeded. Wade smiled. "Now we owe our souls to big money."

"Yup, hundreds of thousands owe their souls, their homes, cars, everything, to banks. Marketing, glamour, glitz, make you believe you need something you don't. When my mother was a kid, her parents bought nothing on credit. If you didn't have the money to buy it outright, you didn't buy it. Not like that anymore."

There was a pause. "Nope, nothing's like that anymore;" then a few moments of silence. "Want to call it quits for now? There's not much more we need to say. You can tell me about which president wanted hard money and which wanted paper, about other conspiracies where people who opposed the Federal Reserve wound up dead, or about wars that made big bankers wealthy, or money that controls our government, but knowing that won't change anything. We can continue to meet as friends, me, you, and Frank. I'd hate to never see you again because we stopped researching."

She considered his comment. "Yes, we can quit, and we can meet as friends, but I have a few more papers to show you before I leave. I'll hold on to the rest."

"Then let's take a break. How about we take this discussion into the living room, have a glass of wine, check the view, and continue there?"

"Sounds good. I could use a change of scenery, a glass of wine, and that imposing view from your window. It's breathtaking."

She gathered whatever papers she had taken from her satchel and followed Wade to the living room, to stand in awe at its spectacular view.

51

DISCUSSION TURNS TO CONSPIRACIES

Wade poured two glasses of wine, then stood before his panoramic view of the city as he used to with Debbie. "I love this view, but it's not the same without her. I think my only salvation is to move."

"Where would you go?"

"No idea. Not someplace drastic like North Carolina, but unless I find someone to make this place special again, warm, and special, I'll leave, maybe to your side of the Hudson."

She shook her head. "That's not such a good idea. Here you walk out of your apartment and you're surrounded by life. Where I am, you meet neighbors when they're walking their dogs or relaxing on their deck. You won't get the 'city that never sleeps' vibrancy you get here."

"Then I'll just have to find someone who makes me feel alive, won't I?" He looked at her with a smile. Stevie hoped he meant it. "So what do you want to show me before you leave?"

"Here." She took a few papers from her satchel. "I mentioned Salmon Chase, but I also found information that involves him, John Wilkes Booth and Lincoln's Secretary of War. Connecting those three people suggests a conspiracy surrounding Lincolns' assassination.

"Then a link that ties JFK's assassination to his opposition of the Federal Reserve. Even if it's wrong, the magic bullet theory our government produced is preposterous."

She pulled another paper from her satchel and placed it on the cocktail table. "This. A congressman in 1983, outspoken against the Fed. He was on a Korean airliner which was 'accidentally' shot down in Soviet airspace. And this: two senators who opposed the Fed shared a similar fate in the 90's, both killed in planes that crashed on consecutive days." She put another paper on the table.

"Then we have Woodrow Wilson, who signed the Federal Reserve Act into law. His 'handler,' Colonel Edward Mandell House, supposedly had strong Zionist connections. Don't think I mentioned that, but tie the Federal Reserve to the deaths of politicians who opposed it, and it sounds like a decades-old fifth column in our country."

Wade nodded, focusing on the papers she was showing him. "Yes, it does . . . sadly."

"Sadness increases exponentially when you realize they succeeded in swaying American opinion who wanted nothing to do with Europe's war, into support for engagement, through ownership and control of the press, my profession, way back then, and sinking the Lusitania.

"People think the Lusitania was a passenger ship, but in reality, she was entered into the Admiralty fleet register as an armed auxiliary cruiser." She handed him information from *Creature from Jekyll Island* that showed the *Lusitania* was listed in *Jane's Fighting Ships* as an auxiliary cruiser, and in the British *Naval Annual,* as an 'armed merchant man.'

"Then the press. I found a quote from the Congressional record in 1917, entered by a representative from Texas; his name was Callaway." She pulled another paper from her satchel, which held so much she sometimes referred to it as her Mary Poppins bag. "Read what he says." She pointed to paragraph two. ". . . that the J.P. Morgan interests, steel, shipbuilding and powder interests, got together twelve men high up in the newspaper world to select the most influential newspapers in the United States to control the policy of the press. They realized it was only necessary to purchase the control of twenty-five of the greatest papers and then," she looked at him to emphasize her next line, "the policy of the papers was bought."

"You memorized this?"

"No, it's not memorized verbatim; I remember what it says. It's on the paper in your hands."

"And you didn't miss a word."

Stevie shrugged. "It just sort of stuck, up here." She pointed to her head."

"Well it 'stuck' perfectly."

"An-y-way, the purpose of these power brokers was to supervise and edit information that was considered vital to the interests *of the purchasers*. That's significant enough for me to remember since it's my profession and since the news succumbs to the same filtering system today."

Wade smiled. Stevie's tenacity made her formidable at her job. Frank must have seen that same quality when she asked him a hundred questions about fracking. If it wasn't clear, she was relentless. He also doubted any other reporter who had seen his grandfather's strongbox and read the note inside would have been so dogged to find out who owns us. "What else?" He asked, knowing she had more to say.

"The sinking of the Lusitania, which may have been a set-up that got us into World War 1 to save England's ass and big bankers' loans. My mind did a fast forward to the World Trade Center attack." She stopped abruptly. "Sorry."

"No, do not apologize. I will read about Wilson and the Lusitania and how big money used, or *caused*, a tragedy to get us into war." Wade took a few gulps of wine, wishing he had something stronger in his glass.

"I'm sorry anyway," Stevie said, "but when you read about it, maybe you'll connect it to how and why the Middle East is now in turmoil, and why the real causes are never taught.

52

ALL OUR CONSPIRACIES

"From what I've read, Wilson wanted Zionist support politically and Zionists wanted U.S. support for the Balfour Declaration. It was a shady deal on both sides, which got us into war, when his campaign promise was to keep us out."

"You showed me the coin that secures the Rothschild relationship with Israel, and it's pretty clear there's a banking connection, but you won't get people to see the World War 1 connection or the politics of the Middle East connection."

"Operation Clean Break shows the politics of the Mid-East connection; Project for a New American Century shows it; and if they read some quotes by Israeli leaders, they might see that our politicians are owned by a cabal. Israel, via AIPAC, an acronym for American Israel Public Affairs Committee, is a major one. Pro-Israel congressmen and women, and senators, accept huge donations from pro-Israel donors, so Israel's agenda often trumps what's best for America. Here, if I can find it . . . . " She flipped through notes, pulled out another file from her satchel and thumbed pages. "October 2001, Ariel Sharon to Shimon Peres, 'I want to tell you something very clear, don't worry about American pressure on Israel, we, the Jewish people control America, and the Americans know it.' As reported on Kol Yisrael radio, which is completely unfamiliar to me."

"Stevie, when you research, you really research. You're like a pit bull. You never let go."

She thought about it. "Maybe, and maybe someday I will let go. I won't spend my life doing this. I want kids, and I'll devote my time to them and Frank. I can't fix what's happened in the past, and I can't bring my fath- . ." She came to an abrupt stop. Wade looked at her and gestured "go on." She changed the subject immediately, a 180 degree turn.

"Anyway, you see the connections I've made, and if people read something other than our controlled press, which intentionally omits who gets government money, how it's spent, and what they do with it, they'd get it too."

"Iraq is a Middle East connection everyone would see if they just looked. It's one small example in the big picture. We invaded because of weapons of mass destruction that weren't there. Ignore the fact Iraq was an Operation Clean Break target, or that they didn't have 'our' kind of central bank until we invaded. Ignore that if it's iffy or controversial. But, do *not* ignore that we invaded and destroyed that country, then got several companies to rebuild it *after* we destroyed it, but the primary one in particular, KBR, Kellogg Brown and Root, a former subsidiary of Halliburton, was once run by our vice-president."

From the sibilant sound that escaped his lips, Stevie knew he didn't know that. "Oh yeah, it was awarded the largest contract by far, close to forty billion, to help rebuild what we destroyed. Our government borrowed money to destroy Iraq, then to rebuild it. Profitable, don't you think?

"Here, look, a mere 750 million of taxpayer money." She passed him photos. "Pictures of the U.S. embassy we built in Iraq for the workers so they can work, eat, relax, shop, whatever." He stared at a huge modern complex with a glass and brown brick façade; then she fanned out the pictures. "This embassy compound is larger than Vatican City; it contains a food court, shopping mall, a six-lane pool for swimming laps, a regular size basketball court, a state-of-the art fitness center and a huge dining room. She slid one picture after another in his direction so he could see the majesty of the complex. "Might there be a connection between big banks and war and," she whispered, "and Israel? One less target for them to bother about in Operation Clean Break?"

Wade leaned back, accepting the magnitude and hopelessness of it all. "No reason to write or print a story about this, Stevie. Readers would think we were insane."

"You're probably right. Our history books don't include this. They've been wiped clean of the past. Like the Lusitania, why was it attacked? Like Woodrow Wilson, who controlled him and what decisions did it affect? Same as today. Who controls publishing houses and the press, and does it matter?" She gave an emphatic nod. "Of course it does. When you control what people read and hear, you control their minds, like *1984*,

Americans are controlled. We're *owned*. We don't get sound information. We're spoon-fed what they want us to believe. Even the Holocaust as justification for Zionists taking Palestine can't be justified.

"Zionists give that as the reason to say they had to have Palestine to save Jews, but that wasn't true. They were offered other countries for refuge that they declined. They wanted Palestine, if they had to bomb the S.S. Patria, killing 267 Jewish passengers to keep Jewish refugees from leaving Palestine, or poison wells and kill Iraqi Jews to frighten them into immigrating to Palestine, their safe haven.

"Zionists ignored European Jews being sent to their deaths. People risked their lives to get messages for help from the World Jewish Congress." She shook her head. "Zionist leaders were concerned about getting Palestine. One leader was quoted as saying one cow in Palestine was more important than all the Jews in Europe, while Jews were being railroaded to death camps."

"I've never read this."

"Here, two articles. Keep them; I'll print myself another copy."

He skimmed the first page. "I keep hearing that being anti-Zionist is being anti-Semitic. What this says indicates the exact opposite." She began gathering her papers. "As much as I don't want to believe any of this, it's here."

"These are documented facts. Zionists will use anyone, any religion, to achieve their goals, and they'll ignore the half million gypsies and at least three million Christians Hitler killed. Several articles I found implicate Zionist collaboration with Nazis, not too hard to find. But Zionists did learn about ethnic cleansing from the Nazis, to rid themselves of a race that stands in the way of their goal. They also learned to attack under the guise of self-defense and to create cataclysmic events to speed their goal along, with cooperative politicians looking the other way. It's global domination, one war at a time, one nation at a time. 9-11 has taken us to hell."

"9-11." His voice was soft. "My wife and child died for a tightly knit global monetary cabal and global control."

"Hundreds of thousands of people have died for a monetary and geopolitical policy that will bring this cabal total control. They care nothing about who dies or what country is destroyed. Fighting terrorism is a perfect euphemism and a perfect cover." She tapped her papers into one thick, neat stack and shoved them into her satchel.

Wade's head drooped. He was lost in the agony of his past. "Stevie, I can't accept that they're gone. I still wake up every morning wondering why I'm here and they're not."

She sighed. "I didn't have first-hand experience, but I can empathize from something deep in my past, and from reading about 9-11 and a cover-up of the attack. I can relate, and I only lived through the torture of writing one story."

"Same story the borough president talked about at the parade?"

She nodded. "Toughest story I ever had to write. Helping pull victims out of rubble, thinking they might survive because of my help; then learning a young mother and her daughter had died on route to the hospital. That killed me."

She glanced up at him. Wade had turned to stone.

233

53

"TELL MY HUSBAND I LOVE HIM"

His hands shook. He could barely speak. "A young mother and her daughter? You pulled out a mother and her daughter who died on their way to St. Vincent's Hospital?"

A chill coursed through her body. Except for the tragedy of two deaths, what did it matter that she had pulled them out or that they had died while being transported to that hospital?

Wade was losing control. His hands balled into fists; his jaw clenched; she heard the grind of his teeth. Suddenly he exploded.

He left his seat, came around the table and grabbed her arm. "And did they, Mrs. Frank Goring," he shouted, his voice filled with hate, "by any chance, look like this?" Long strides took him to his wife's picture with Stevie in tow. He halted in front of it and slammed his fist against the frame, cracking it. Ignoring that, he turned to his right.

234

"And by any chance, did the face of that little girl look like this?" He pounded against Ryan's picture, so hard it slammed against the wall, bounced off and hit the floor.

He seethed, turning towards her with hatred in his eyes. "Did they, Stevie? Did they look like that? And did that last line you used that clinched your story, and your new job, say, "Tell my husband I love him"?

Stevie froze. That was it; that was the line, but how did he know, then suddenly, "Oh my God!" She uttered. "That was your wife and your child?"

"My wife, Debbie; my child, Ryan. My life, everything I lived for, and you used them to get yourself a job!"

"What?" Stevie was shocked. "No . . . no! I never used them or anyone to get a job. How can you think that? I had no idea who they were; no one did. I was just a reporter doing my job, covering one of the worst tragedies this nation has ever seen, and covering it from a first-hand perspective. I was down there!"

"But *you* didn't die there! They did! They died! That killed me, and you got a great job out of it!"

"What are you saying, Wade, that I wrote sensationalism to get a promotion or a better job?"

His face was livid, filled with rage. He had become a monster. She backed up, frightened, each step closer to the door as he inched towards her.

He spoke softly, his voice exuding hatred. "I always said if I ever found the reporter who had the gall to expose something so personal for me, I'd kill him. I thought it was a guy; never put the name together with a woman, but it doesn't matter. I hated you when you were an image, and I hate you now. Those words were meant for me, not the world. My wife's last words saying she loved me! You are a bitch, an insensitive bitch. Get out!"

Tears ran down her face. Something so traumatic for him and for her, too, had become an avatar of hate, but she gathered whatever courage she could muster and faced him. How dare he think that of her, after all they'd been through together?

"My intent was to write the best story and convey the most accurate details of the tragedy I could. Your wife looked up at me, into my eyes, pleading, telling me to tell her husband she loved him. I didn't know who she was. I didn't know who you were, or that you were her husband. But I do know that had it *not* been for me writing your wife's last words, you would *never* have known what they were!"

She jerked her arm from his grasp and raced out the door, her satchel locked under her arm. She'd ask for Stan at the desk. If he didn't respond, she'd find her own way home. Amidst tears, she'd make it home.

54

STEVIE'S NIGHTMARE UNRAVELS

S tan was waiting for her at the front entrance. She threw herself into the limo as he held the door open. The ride home was torture. Dark silhouetted clouds drifted across a setting sun, making the world bleaker than hers already was. Stan offered a few comments meant to be consolation, but statements like "He doesn't mean to take it out on you," and, "You can't take it personally," alleviated nothing. Yes, he did take it out on her and yes it was personal because she had written the story. She cried from Wade's apartment to her house, to her phone. She prayed Frank answered.

His, "Hi, Babe, vaporized when he heard her tears and a few incoherent words between sobs. "He threw you out? Is he crazy?" Anger and his protective instincts surfaced instantly. "I'm coming home. Be there in less than an hour."

"No, don't drive . . ." but he had already hung up.

He was home in record time. No way he was driving at sixty-five miles an hour. 95N all the way to the Lincoln Tunnel, a distance of sixty miles, would have taken a minimum of an hour had he been the only car on the road, and that was impossible. Frank swung open the door at 7:44, forty-nine minutes after he had hung up.

Stevie was nowhere on the first floor, not the living room, family room, dining room or kitchen. Whimpering came from upstairs. He took the stairs three at the time. There she was, on the bed in a fetal position, sobbing into her pillow. He wrapped his arms around her. She turned to him and sobbed into his chest, clutching something solid to her breast.

"Hon, it's okay. Don't let him hurt you like this."

"It's not just Wade," she choked on tears. "It's memories from my past. I understand his grief because I lived it, but he thinks I wrote that last line for a job. I wish someone had written my father's last words so I could have read them. What was he thinking when he was killed? Was he thinking of my mother? Was he thinking of me?"

She cried uncontrollably. Finally she was telling him about her dad. Frank cradled her gently. "Your dad?" He whispered, touching the picture frame she clutched tightly. She nodded. "May I see?" He held a corner of the frame and she let him take it. He turned it slowly, recognizing its reverence.

The photo showed a handsome man in a bathing suit with an adorable blond-haired child hoisted on his shoulders, splashing through the surf. His little girl was laughing, reaching up to clutch low-flying seagulls. Frank smiled to see his wife as a child, exuding happiness, being part of nature, loving life, yet he was overcome with sadness. This was Stevie with her father before he had been killed. How, where, she had yet to say, but a feeling of universal sadness washed over him as he thought of life, death and what and why something takes it from us.

He had never felt so much love as he did this moment. Stevie had opened up, even a little, at last. He held her tightly while she released years of sorrow, until sorrow surrendered to sleep, *sleep that knits up the raveled sleeve of care*. He covered her with her favorite blanket, put her father's picture on her dresser, then tiptoed out.

55

FRANK'S GUILT

In the morning, he showered and dressed before she awoke. His note said he was starting for work. He'd call her later. He loved her more than anything, and if she needed to talk, call him, anytime.

As he drove, he had time to reflect on the night, the few words that had passed between them and references Stevie had made before about never allowing herself to get serious with men. She had said she had always kept her father's picture in her dresser to try and overcome the specter of his death and a wall that kept her from love. She was always running. When he asked her why, she said that if her dad had been taken, the man she loved might be taken too.

"What about me? You married me," he had said.

She snuggled in closer and yawned. "Because of that night on my porch."

Her words stuck in his head all night, while he showered in the morning and now, as he drove to work.

She was telling him that night on her porch was the first time she had been with a man.

He dreaded the thought that it was true, because if it were, then that perfect night for him must have been a nightmare for her. He had gotten in his truck and left, left her alone, without a soft word, or a loving arm to hold her.

Ironic that in his mature years, he had considered himself to be a thoughtful person, considerate of people's feelings. That image had just shattered. He had thought of his own desires, while Stevie, that naïve, young woman he had cavalierly left to fend off a masher at Ribs and Brew, had been left to deal with trauma alone.

He was angry at Wade too. Had it not been for his outburst, his wife's emotional turmoil would not have surfaced. But maybe in another way, it was a blessing in disguise. At least Stevie had talked, even a little. He was glad he had left her his note, two notes. The first said, "Call me, anytime;" the second, taped to the bathroom mirror, said, "Love you forever." He hoped that would account for something.

241

56

GROUNDBREAKING
CEREMONY

The ceremony's setting was the same, but the tone and mood were different. When she had covered America Remembers, 9-11, a year after the attack, family and relatives of victims were still reeling from disbelief, shock, uncertainty of pulling their lives together.

Every victim's name had been read aloud and consecrated to eternity, some names she knew; they had been her friends. Loved ones placed flowers in the Circle of Honor, mayors, former mayors, and governors spoke about the horrific acts of terror.

New York City's mayor read Lincoln's Gettysburg Address. When he finished with ". . . that we here highly resolve that these dead shall not have died in vain—that this nation, under God, shall have a new birth of freedom—and that government of the people, by the people, for the people, shall not perish from the earth," all eyes were heavy with tears.

Now, almost five years later, as somber as ceremonies would always be, this one was about a rebirth of life, a sense of resolve and a new birth of freedom manifesting itself at Ground Zero. July 4, 2006, the cornerstone was being laid, and Stevie was there to cover it. Without acknowledging him, so was Wade, sitting on the dais, second row. He saw her, but neither made contact.

At this moment, his heart hated her more than he thought he could hate anyone, despite logic telling him his hatred was misplaced. She had done nothing to cause the 9-11 attack that took his wife and child, and nothing to intentionally hurt him. But he had to hate someone; so he made her and her story his target.

He watched as she took notes, copied key words from the governor's speech, her recorder for backup. His words were moving: ". . . today we lay the cornerstone for a new symbol of this city and this country . . ." his last words were of resolve to triumph in the face of terror.

The huge cornerstone crafted from Adirondack granite was positioned onto its bed; then its drape was removed. On it was written, "To honor and remember those who lost their lives on September 11, 2001 and as a tribute to the enduring spirit of freedom."

Emotional and moving. She took notes with alacrity, listening and digesting every spoken word, trying to feel each family's pain, as though it would help. It would remind her of her father, and yes, that would help her write a better story.

When the ceremony ended, Jim Farley cornered her. "Wish we could retrace the last five years so we could have prevented this tragedy."

"I wish we could retrace the last twenty-three." But he had no idea what she was talking about, and she didn't offer to explain.

She bid him goodbye and started for home where Frank was waiting. He had wanted to go with her so Wade's presence wouldn't rattle her, but she insisted she could do it, and she had. She had been courageous in the face of unfounded rejection from a man she had trusted and warmed to.

Maybe someday she'd be able to tell him that she had experienced tragedy from war too, but all she wanted at this moment was a warm shower and the steak Frank would be grilling on this July 4th. She felt blessed, and she prayed someone would come along and fill Wade's life as Frank had filled hers.

57

GROUNDBREAKING STORY

She included the Freedom Tower's height. With the spire, it reached 1,776 feet high. Impressive and symbolic of freedom, but she did not include anything about the World Trade Center attack or Buildings 1, 2, and 7, that third building that just happened to come down because a little fire had supposedly jumped from its two sister buildings. Things like molten, liquid steel pouring from collapsed buildings as though fuel could melt them; the owner of building seven saying he told his crew to "pull it" even though it had been hit by nothing; three buildings of reinforced steel pancaking as though they had been detonated – as much as she wanted to include them, those things she left out.

She was naïve about life, but not about government machinations. If our government acknowledged the facts she was omitting, that would mean . . . not a surprise attack. According to experts, explosive charges took anywhere from two to fourteen weeks to be set. Would she even imply someone knew those buildings were coming down? Not in this story; this article would be a tribute to the victims and their families, nothing else, and that's how she wrote it.

Her story made the paper Wednesday, July 5th. Jim Farley called to say great job, and to tell her the council had approved funding for his project.

58

LEBANON ATTACK
IMMINENT

She was exhausted, but antsy. It was Friday afternoon and Jeffrey had just summoned her into his office. Everyone was wrapping up for the weekend, Lara was giggling and gabbing about another date she had had with a guy who made her laugh. "On his phone all night?" Stevie teased.

"Not once. He's my brother's *other* friend, a guy from work."

She not only had a good time, but they were going out tomorrow, dinner and tickets to "Jersey Boys."

Jeffrey had said five minutes. She glanced at her watch; that meant now. She left her desk and walked to his office. He motioned her to sit; then glanced down at his notes while she studied patterns on the ceiling, impatient for him to begin. Home was all she could think about, getting stuck in traffic, and Frank getting there before she could leave.

"What do you know about Sheba'a Farms?"

"In Lebanon?" Jeffrey nodded. "It could also be in Syria, depending on who you ask. Lebanon has always claimed it; some Lebanese have deeds in their names or their parents' names. Israel claims it's part of the Golan, which they occupy, and Syria claims that land belongs to Lebanon. Seems the U.N. drew a map and divided it incorrectly. Typical of colonial expansion, carving up the Mid-East based on what they know, don't know, or don't want to know.

"It's a sore point, though, because if it's in Syria, Israel uses that as justification to continue its occupation there. If it's in Lebanon, they're supposed to get out." She threw up her hands with a look saying, "Whose gonna fix this mess?" "Why did you ask that?"

"I told you a while ago there was some saber rattling in that area." Jeffrey recounted a brief discussion they had had a while back. "Now there's a lot more activity going on there across the border. Looks like we're getting that invasion we had hinted at before. If you want the story when, not 'if' in my opinion, that attack comes, you've got it."

Another invasion of Lebanon; another pro-Israel perspective story. Did she want to do it the mainstream media way?

"Foreign correspondents will send enough details about military aspects, and if you don't want my red pen slashing your copy, make it a human interest article."

She thought about that. His last sentence was meant to remind her she had said she'd cover the story if he didn't slash too much from her Gaza story. But she had given him the whitewashed version after he balked at the gutsy one.

How much of this story would he cut, because she wasn't going to sanitize it, not about a war from the country that had caused her father's death.

"I can do that. A human interest story will allow more flexibility, but I'm not submitting two drafts for this one, Jeffrey."

"And why is that?" He glared at her.

"I have my reasons. You'll know depending on how I write it. I'll include quotes from the Lebanese-Americans I spoke to when I interviewed for the Gaza story, and beginning next week, I'll interview more. I'll also include a little history, go back to Israel's first Lebanon invasion in 1978. Maybe I'll go back as far 1948, when Zionists drove out the Palestinians and they fled to Jordan and Lebanon. I'll be discreet and professional, but I'm gonna include the facts, no sugar coating to save Israel's image." She hesitated; then added. "In time people will know that image can never be saved."

Jeffrey blanched. "Stevie, I've always known you to be candid, but not this candid. What's gotten into you?"

She shook her head. "Nothing. This is just one topic I won't compromise on. I'll leave it to you to delete what you want."

"Okay, do the story your way and I'll cut it mine."

"Since you're positive a war is imminent, I won't start another story. I'll stick with research for this."

He rapped his pencil against his desk. "Okay, that makes sense. No reason to wait since all foreign correspondents say it's a done deal."

59

CHILDHOOD PAIN

She rethought her decision as soon as she left Jeffrey's office.

Since she was four, she had never talked about her father or the place where he had been killed. Neighborhood friends she had played with knew, but once she started school, nothing. When kids talked about their dads, she'd shrink back and hide. Every now and again, some newcomer would ask why her dad was never there, were her parents divorced; was he dead. If it got that far, a knowing classmate would kick that kid or poke her in the ribs, indicating shut up. So could she write this now?

She wasn't a kid anymore, but even when she had shown Frank her dad's picture, how or where he had been killed never came up, and by next morning, he had gone. Since the topic would never be an over-the-phone conversation, she'd have to let it play out naturally. She'd tell him if he asked; otherwise, she'd see how she dealt with this upcoming story. That would be the real test.

Time would do the telling, and that time would be soon. But until then, she had research to do and more Lebanese-Americans to interview.

60

LEBANESE-AMERICANS
CONDEMN INVASION

Monday morning and Stevie was back in the Arabic section of the city for more interviews with Lebanese-Americans. Her questions were poignant, as were the replies.

"We write about the aid Syria or Iran gives Hezbollah for missiles that it fires into Israel, but do we write about aid we give Israel that lets it invade countries it has no right to invade?" Dr. Azar did not equivocate. "We go after the Middle East countries that have not capitulated to the U.S. or Israel. We make it easy to attack them because we label them terrorists, which we define as anyone who opposes Israel, a state that has broken the conditions it agreed upon when it applied for statehood."

"What about the argument that it's the only democracy in the Middle East?" She asked.

"Iran was a democracy in the early 50's under Mossadegh, but we deposed him because he nationalized his oil industries. We don't care about democracies, only power, money and Israel, a state that doesn't come close to being a democracy. It is an apartheid state, destroying and massacring at will.

"In the twenty-five years between 1948 and the early 1970's, in Palestine's fifteen districts, Israel destroyed 385 villages out of its 475, their inhabitants massacred, women, children, all massacred. Have you read that?" Stevie shook her head. This she had not read. "And, since January of last year until now, Israel has destroyed 664 Palestinian homes? Did you know this, Ms. Komsky?"

"No, doctor, I did not."

He shook his head in dismay. "And now Israel is going after Lebanon for the third time, purportedly because Hezbollah captured two IDF soldiers, but this attack had been planned for years. If it hadn't been for this reason, they would have found another." He faced her squarely. "Please, Ms. Komsky, do more research . . . and print the truth."

She left in a stupor. She had been researching Israel's aggression for years and knew it was its third Lebanon invasion, but she had never read the number of Palestinian villages it had destroyed. *Do more research? He's kidding, right?*

Her next interviews were with two shop owners, Tariq and John. "So, it appears the U.S. outcry is that Syria and Iran are supplying Hezbollah," Tariq said. "So what? Where's the outcry that the billions we give Israel buys them weapons that destroy the country of my parents? Is it only horrific when a country other than us supplies a country with weapons? Has your paper ever written about the origins of the conflict early in the 1900's, when

Zionists massacred peaceful, unarmed Palestinians, then invaded our country to hunt down the PLO that wasn't there?"

John agreed. "Does anyone here know about Dier Yassin, the 1948 massacre which began the Palestinian exodus? Have they even heard the name? Seven-hundred fifty thousand Palestinians fled into Jordan and our country, because Israel massacred that village, which created an imbalance and caused our civil war. The second part of the Balfour Declaration stated that nothing should be done that may prejudice the civil and religious rights of existing non-Jewish communities in Palestine . . ." Does it look like Israel read that part?" He was correct. The U.S., Israel and the press rewrote the past and buried documents showing Israel's horrific crimes against humanity.

Both men condemned our government and our complicit press, but their harsh criticism of Israel and our country's arbitrary support for its illegal acts did not prevent them from giving her so much food it would last her days, meat pies, string cheese, which Frank loved, and a dozen loaves of pita bread. Her shoulder satchel leaned.

Sam owned a men's fashion store several blocks down. "Your press writes in the pejorative about aid Syria or Iran gives Hezbollah for resisting invading Israelis. At the same time, we praise the forces in Poland, France, and other European countries that resisted the Nazis who occupied their countries. Hezbollah and Hamas are the resistance that has sprung from the ashes of occupation. They arose to fight an invading, occupying power. The irony is that the occupying power here claims it's the victim while the occupied countries that try to resist are attacked and blockaded by Israel and its benefactor, the U.S. We should be ashamed."

Her heart broke for these people. *Might does make right.* Despondent, she started home. More another day.

And so it went, to the end of the week, as the Lebanon invasion began and Israel bombed civilian targets, bridges, power systems, Red Cross ambulances, as Hezbollah valiantly defended its country. She had newspapers from a full week and pages of research which took her back to 1948, Zionists slanting the press, conniving UN member nations to vote yes for the state of Israel, and pressuring Truman to recognize it. He did, eleven minutes later.

Exhausted, she made a cup of tea and climbed the stairs to review history in her room. She worked over an hour, reviewing notes, then stopped at Sunday morning, October 23, 1983, when terrorists bombed the Marine barracks in Beirut, killing 241 U.S. and 68 French military personnel. Two hundred forty she did not know, but that "one" she did; it had been her father, blown apart by the explosion, with his last breath, trying to pull his commanding officer to safety. That "one" had been a mere statistic on paper, but a forever nightmare for her. Her father, a statistic that had devastated her life and her mother's. Did she understand Wade's grief? You bet she did.

She shut 1983 out of her mind and closed her folders. She'd review more Monday. Frank would be home in less than an hour. It was time to put the past in the past and leave the weekend for him.

61

STEVIE GETS READY TO WRITE

Early Monday morning her computer keys began to click before she showered and dressed for work. Frank forced himself out of bed an hour earlier than his usual time because shore traffic had gone into peak summertime mode, jamming roads earlier. He needed an extra hour to have a smooth drive.

By the time he was dressed, Stevie was downstairs making him breakfast – wet scrambled eggs with cheese, toast with butter and blueberry preserves, and two sausage links diced into bite-sized pieces. With such attention, he didn't want to leave, especially as Stevie lilted around the kitchen wearing a 4X T-shirt that stopped just above her knees. She was sexier in that than in a tight pair of jeans.

"If I didn't have to work," he said, swallowing his last bite of eggs and giving her his last wedge of toast, "you'd be upstairs with me and you wouldn't be typing."

"But you *do* have to work, and I do have to write. This story is going to be complex. I need an outline and I have to start it while the ideas are still fresh in my mind. So you go to work, I run upstairs to get in some typing and we'll simply have to be stoic until Friday." She finished the toast as she walked him to the door and kissed him goodbye. He leaned her against the lintel and kissed her with passion. "Be ready," he whispered.

She kissed him back. "I am always ready."

Frank pushed himself away and headed for his truck. Stevie stood in the doorway, watching her sexy husband hop in, back out the drive, and head for the highway.

Friday couldn't come too soon. She hurried upstairs to start an outline before she had to leave for work.

62

STEVIE'S STORY BLASTS INVASION

She was fusing past with present for this story. It would be informative, yet human interest. She had facts from the past and present that would make this a powerful story. It would tell the truth about the past that had steered Israel's invasions, our foreign policy, and our Middle East wars.

"Hear no evil; see no evil. We turn our backs on Israel's past aggressions, its continuous settlements in Palestine, its demolition of Palestinian homes, lands, olive groves, farms, hospitals, soccer fields, because Israel has the right to defend itself. In defiance of the Geneva Convention and dozens of UN resolutions, which we veto, Israel has the right to defend itself when no country has attacked it. It forgets it has no right as an invading country to settle lands it seizes, and we forget to remind it because Israel is an exception. Israel is our special friend, our fifty-first state; it has always had impunity.

"Would it matter if Congress knew about Sabra and Shatila? Would it matter if they've heard about Deir Yassin? "Deir Yassin, a peaceful Palestinian village that had been promised security by a Zionist faction during the Arab-Zionist hostilities when Palestinians were losing their lands to Zionists. Despite this promise, Deir Yassin was destroyed, its unarmed citizens massacred in their homes and on the streets, a bloodbath conveniently forgotten. Forgotten intentionally for the world, but not by Menachem Begin in *The Revolt*, 'Without what was done at Deir Yassin there would not have been a state of Israel ... The Arabs began fleeing in panic, shouting 'Deir Yassin.' Begin knew what they had done.

"Moshe Dayan also makes it clear that there were more Deir Yassins. In his address at the Haifa Technion University, which Ha'aretz quoted in 1969, he states, 'Jewish villages were built in the place of Arab villages. You do not even know the names of these Arab villages, and I do not blame you because geography books no longer exist, not only do the books not exist, the Arab villages are not there either. Nahlal arose in the place of Mahlul; Kibbutz Gvat in the place of Jibta; Kibbutz Sarid in the place of Huneifis; and Kefar Yehushu'a in the place of Tal al-Shuman. There is not one single place built in this country that did not have a former Arab population.' And on it goes, as villagers were no match for Zionist organization, skill, and arms.

"After Deir Yassin, Palestinians fled to Jordan and Lebanon, lighting the kindling for decades of unsuccessful resistance and the emergence of the PLO in Jordan which caused demographic imbalances and turmoil. After Jordan drove the PLO out, they fled to Lebanon, where another imbalance was created, after which Arafat and the PLO left for Tunisia. Lebanon was free of the PLO, but using the justification that its purpose was to root out PLO stragglers, Israel invaded anyway.

"To understand this, examine Israel's objective, from the UN Security Council Official Records, April 19, 1982, which quotes an article in Ha'aretz from March 25, 1975: '. . . We shall determine which Arab move is, from our point of view, a *casus belli* and at what point we shall play the game differently from the way others expect us to. If the free world is frightened and the West is in the process of decline, it may be that we have a number of means available to terrorize it more than the Arabs would. A word to the wise is enough'.

"A warning to the West? Sounds like it, and still our Congress ignores, turns its back, hides. Genuflecting to Israel has become our way of life. In exchange, politicians get favorable press, money, power, and votes. They get reelected. American citizens get war, our dead young men, despair, and debt.

"Post-World War II, Germany granted the right of return to expatriated Jews, yet Israel refuses that same right of return to Palestinians. Instead, it imports more settlers to take more land. Hypocrisy is like a dead carcass rotting in sun – it stinks. Americans have never been given an accurate picture of Israel's carnage in the Middle East, in Palestine or in Lebanon, with attacks in 1978, 1982, and now.

"Now, why now? Now, because Israel still occupies Southern Lebanon's territory, Sheba'a Farms, because the UN can't draw a line, a simple Blue Line to delineate where Southern Lebanon ends and northern Israel begins.

260

You don't put Sheba'a farms in the Golan when it clearly belongs in Lebanon, but the UN did. As a result, there have been border raids, with Hezbollah claiming Israel still occupies part of its country and it should leave.

"Cross-border raids over the Blue Line have been frequent, but they have not been equal; In the past six years, it's been more than a ten to one ratio: Hezbollah commits one; Israel commits ten, maybe twelve. This Wednesday, July 12, Hezbollah initiated the raid. It crossed into Israel, attacked an IDF patrol, killed three IDF soldiers and captured two. Hezbollah's intention is to use the captured soldiers for a prisoner swap - the two IDF soldiers for the release of Lebanese prisoners Israel has held for years.

"Israel's response has been air, naval and ground attacks as Hezbollah counter-attacks with hundreds of rockets into northern Israel, some reaching as far as Haifa. Using an Iranian-made unmanned drone, Hezbollah has also damaged an Israeli warship off Lebanon's coast. Israel's strategy is to bomb anywhere and everywhere - Hezbollah's arms suppliers, Lebanon's citizens, and its infrastructure - with weapons the U.S. has given it to be used only for self-defense.

"For self-defense. This is not self-defense. This is an attack planned long ago awaiting an excuse to begin, because, according to sources, Israel began to prepare for war against Hezbollah six years ago and has simulated and rehearsed its attack for the last two. This implies that, had it not been for Hezbollah's capture of two IDF soldiers, Israel would have found another reason to invade, and her past aggressions substantiate this motive: decimate Lebanon and its only protector, Hezbollah."

Stevie wrapped up her story with quotes from her interviews. Dr. Azar's quote about destruction of villages, Sam showing U.S. hypocrisy by supporting resistance against Hitler's invasion and condemning it for Hamas and Hezbollah, and Tariq and John's condemnation of our complicit press for not printing the real causes of the hostilities, she interpolated into her story. Omitting the truth and their quotes is something she would never do. Jeffrey might slash them, but she'd write the truth.

Monday had blended into Tuesday when she finished her story. She organized her desk before she left work and she'd do the same with her notes at home. Tomorrow, she'd write her epilogue.

63

"I AM FOUR"

*M*ommy took me to the mall this morning to buy decorations and favors for my birthday party. It's next week; I will be five. We plop our bags on the coffee table and hurry to the kitchen for something to eat. We are starving.

Mommy gets peanut butter and blueberry jam from the fridge and I get bread. Mom slices apple wedges. She says they're high in Vitamin C. We eat, I help Mommy clear the table. We hurry because Daddy always calls early Sunday afternoon. I sit on the sofa, waiting for Daddy's call, reading my favorite book, "The Night Before Christmas." Even though it's not Christmas, it reminds me of the last time I saw my dad.

I can read almost the entire book myself, except for a few words Mom has to help me with. I've been practicing, so next time Dad comes home, I can read it to him all by myself. Dad says he might be home for Christmas. I can't wait to see him. I miss Daddy so much.

I run upstairs to pull Daddy's picture down from my dresser and hug him tight. The picture is of me on Daddy's shoulders the summer I was three. We are at the beach. Daddy is running through the surf and I am reaching up to catch a seagull. One flies so close I almost touch it.

Mommy calls me downstairs to help her get ready for Daddy's call. She is clearing the table and washing dishes. The doorbell rings. I rush to the door to see who is there. "Mommy, men are at the door."

Mommy shuts the faucet and opens the door. Three men stand there, wearing uniforms like Daddy wears. They mumble something; I can't hear, but it must have been bad because Mommy puts her hands to her mouth and screams. She keeps screaming. I hold on to her leg; she falls. The men help Mommy to the sofa. Mommy is shrieking and holding me. She tells them to leave. "Get out," she screams. "Get out!" She keeps screaming. I am scared.

The men put papers on the table and leave. Mommy cries; she runs to the bedroom and collapses on the bed, still shrieking. Jenny's mom opens the door and peeks in; then she goes into Mommy's room and runs to her side. She holds her and Mommy cries into her shoulder.

She tells me Mommy will be all right in time. Mommy doesn't look at her; she doesn't stop crying. She asks if Mommy wants her to take me to her house so I can be with Jenny. Mommy shakes her head yes. Jenny's mom takes my hand and we leave. She is crying too.

Mommy cries all day and next day. She cries every day; she doesn't leave the house; she doesn't eat. Neighbors tiptoe in and leave us food. Jenny's mom says I can stay with her; I go every day. I go there for my birthday, too. My friends are there, but Mommy doesn't come. I want to ask Mommy why Daddy doesn't call, but Jenny's mom says my mom will tell me when she can. Give Mommy a little more time.

After my party, Mommy holds me and says she's sorry. She's sorry she wasn't at my party, but she would have ruined it for me by crying. Then she tells me why Daddy didn't call. She tells me he'll never call again. I ask her if he's mad at me. She hugs me harder and says no. She tells me Daddy will always love me, but he can't call because he went to heaven.

I ask Mommy where heaven is. She says no one really knows, but good people go there when they die. My daddy was a real good person & a great dad; so that's where he is. I miss him. I will always miss him, and I will do my best to be a good person so I go there when I die and see Daddy again.

I want my daddy; I want him here with me, but he never will be. Mommy tells me he was killed when some bad people caused an explosion where Daddy was staying. Mommy says she will try to be the same person she was before Daddy died. But she never was. Neither was I.

I grew up without my dad because of a war. I didn't know anything about war then, but I do now. I remember my mother telling me war is a monster, a greedy, evil monster that feeds on good people because it can.

That's what my mother told me then, and I believed her. Now that I'm grown, I still believe her – war is an evil monster that feeds on good people because it can. Only difference is that now, I know that monster has a name.

Stevie ended her story while tears were running down her cheeks. She had kept her feelings to herself for decades, not even telling her mother. It was only now she had come face to face with it, after falling in love with Frank and getting to know Wade and his tragedy. Writing this story and her epilogue had been cathartic for her. She felt as though her own incubus had been lifted off her back. She would run no longer.

64

STEVIE SUBMITS LEBANON
STORY

Thursday morning drifted into late afternoon by the time Stevie submitted her story and its epilogue. Not that she couldn't have completed it yesterday, but Jeff had sent her to cover a 20k run in Central Park whose proceeds would refurbish a children's center near the Village. Lara was in Salem County, New Jersey, doing a follow-up piece on nuclear power plant safety, and Jeff's other go-to reporter was sick.

That pushed Stevie's schedule back a day, but it was of no consequence; the Israeli invasion showed no signs of abating. Her story would be topical for at least another two weeks, much longer, unless the UN intervened with a cease-fire agreement of some kind.

Shortly after 4:00, Stevie walked her story, "Israel Invades Lebanon, Again," over to Jeff's office, where she knocked out of courtesy, walked in, and sat. When his door was open, it was open-admittance to everyone.

Jeffrey looked up from scrutinizing a letter he was reading. "From the top brass," he said, flicking the letter in his hand, "checking a few odds and ends. Trivia," he added, obviously disgruntled with its content. He turned to her. "So the story is done. Will I like it?" He put out his hand as Stevie passed four pages to him.

Stevie sighed. "You may like it, but more than likely you'll cut it."

"Too long?"

Stevie looked at him askance. "I wrote the truth."

It was his turn to look askance. "And what way is that?"

"The truth, the way the press should have written articles about Israel decades ago; so we would not have gotten sucked into wars we never should have been in or that could have resolved easily if we had just told Israel, 'No more money until u go back to your pre - '67 borders & allow Palestine its sovereign state and refugees the right of return.' That's the way I wrote it, like journalism is supposed to be."

Jeffrey's pencil top thumped his desk, one thump, then another and another, until Stevie could hear a rhythm in its beat. She waited. No reason to rush an answer. It would come when Jeffrey was ready and nothing she said would change it.

"Okay," he said with finality, "Leave it; I'll read it; I'll cut whatever I want. It's done. Start covering some summer festivities and political campaigns. I think Jim Farley is planning a summer fundraiser early August."

That was her cue. She nodded and left his office. She was done for the day. She collected her things and started for home. The day was hot; she was tired. She'd take the ferry.

65

BACKLASH

She was exceptionally early. Not that she had set her alarm an hour earlier, but she couldn't get much sleep. Frank had called later than usual, and they had talked well past midnight. But as tired as she thought she was, she tossed all night. By 4:30, she was in the shower. By 5:30, she was on the bus.

Sipping her second cup of coffee, she walked into work to an exceptionally quiet morning. At first, she thought the few colleagues that were there at this hour were tired, like her. But something didn't feel right. What was wrong? Had she missed something? When she got to her desk, she saw the morning issue, banner headline, "Israel Invades Lebanon, Again." *Oh, no.* She glanced around. Everyone was reading her story.

She dropped her things, put down her coffee and raced through the article, skimming one paragraph at a time. Jeffrey had cut nothing. It was all intact, just as she had written it.

She picked up the issue and hurried to Jeff's office. The door was open, no change in that, but there was a change in his routine - he was not sitting behind his desk. Instead, he was packing everything on his desk into two large boxes – photos, staplers, pencil sharpener, papers, and files.

"Jeffrey?" She asked with apprehension, hesitant to hear the answer. "Are you packing for the reason I think you are packing?"

"It was resign or be fired. I chose being fired – I get to collect unemployment. Hell, I've paid into it for decades. May as well get some benefit."

"Because of my story?" He nodded. "Oh, Jeffrey, I'm so sorry."

"I expected it. I had gotten backlash after your Operation Clean Break story, much more after your Gaza article. I knew if I printed your article about Lebanon, it would be a make or break issue."

"But you printed it anyway? Why?"

He motioned her to take a seat, then moved one of the boxes blocking his center view and sat. "Decades ago when I was a young reporter, I was idealistic, a bit like you. I thought my job was to seek and print the truth, that that was the objective in journalism." He snickered and shook his head. "Have you heard of a woman named Dorothy Thompson?"

"Name sounds familiar, but I've never researched anything about her, so my answer is no."

"Dorothy Thompson was a very famous, very well-known journalist, whose face had been on the cover of *Time* magazine. Originally, she supported Zionism, but after the war she visited the Middle East and began speaking against the atrocities of Jewish terrorism. A relentless, orchestrated attack against her character and her career followed. She was dropped by the *Post*, owned by Jacob Schiff's granddaughter; dropped by everyone else – speaking engagements, radio program - all gone. In time, history was erased, and the past, as it had actually occurred, was gone. 'Who controls the present control the past.' Orwell was right."

"Similar to what I had learned about big bankers identifying twelve major papers that would have to be bought for the public's mind to be brainwashed about entering World War 1. Maybe worse for Thompson, an excellent journalist, destroyed because she printed the truth."

"That's why I printed your article. I kept you in tow to a degree and, had I not read your epilogue, I would have slashed your story." His head drooped. "After I read your epilogue, I couldn't. You had said there was a reason you couldn't write about the Middle East . . . now I know why. Stevie, I am so sorry." He looked up. There were tears in his young reporter's eyes. "Now I understand what our complicit press has done to individuals I care about. Your epilogue brought it all home."

She was reliving her father's death in staccato frames, until she realized how her story had devastated her editor's life and his career. "But Jeffrey, you lost your job. You have a wife, three kids and a mortgage. I wish you had slashed it."

"Not to fear." He rose from his seat, somewhat elated. "I have another job." She looked at him in awe. "I followed up on a few calls yesterday. A college roommate who publishes a men's health magazine has wanted my 'expertise' for years. I finally said yes. A tad less pay, but nothing significant, and he publishes from Hoboken – a travel savings right there."

A sigh of relief, then Stevie asked, "Who's taking your place?"

"Ah, yes, good question and a topic you need to know. You won't like him. He's hard core, won't give you an inch of leeway. It's your decision. I wrote a letter, on official stationery, firing you. I wrote it yesterday in anticipation of this outcome. You can stay, work here under his terms, or take the letter to unemployment and collect while you're looking for another job. Up to you. My recommendation is to take the letter – it's in your center drawer – and find something you'll enjoy, because I doubt you'll enjoy working for him. He won't fire you, but he'll make you squirm to the point where you'll quit."

"That bad huh?"

Jeffrey nodded. She could never work for a mean person. A hardliner, maybe, but not mean. She understood why Jeff had written her dismissal letter. Then an idea popped into her head. "Jeffrey, has your friend ever considered adding a woman's section to his men's health magazine?"

"Hmmm, you mean include a caret in the title so it reads, *Mens* - insert caret – *& Women's Health*? Not a bad idea. I'll run it by him and let you know. So, go on, get out of here. I've got lots of packing to do." He glanced around his office. "The things you can accumulate in fifteen years."

Stevie rose, walked around Jeff's desk, and kissed his cheek. "I would work for you anytime."

66

FRANK REACTS

It was past 1:00 when Frank sat back with a coffee and an apple, feet up on his desk, newspaper on his lap. He had analyzed computer feed all morning, comparing production of various sites and was happy, but not surprised, to see Bradford County surpassing projected output. Gary was following in his footsteps as Frank knew he would.

So, relaxed, and ready to read, he smiled with pride when he saw his wife's story on the front page. She was a great writer; destined for that coveted spot someday. He didn't anticipate it would have been this soon. Nor did he anticipate the epilogue that was to follow.

The story was great. Stevie addressed Israel's invasion head on, no holds barred, with insight and detailed research for backup. She had worded it skillfully, interpolating quotes from her Lebanese-American interviewees adroitly, achieving maximum effect. It was an excellent article which he was certain would elicit backlash of some sort. In fact, Frank wondered why Jeffrey hadn't cut several paragraphs.

Epilogue? What's this? Then he began to read: ". . . *Mommy calls me downstairs to help her get ready for Daddy's call. She is clearing the table and washing dishes. The doorbell rings. I rush to the door to see who is there. "Mommy, men are at the door."*

Mommy shuts the faucet and opens the door. Three men stand there, wearing uniforms like Daddy wears. They mumble something; I can't hear, but it must have been bad because Mommy puts her hands to her mouth and screams. She keeps screaming. I hold on to her leg; she falls. The men help Mommy to the sofa. Mommy is shrieking and holding me. She tells them to leave. "Get out," she screams. "Get out!" She keeps screaming. I am scared.

The men put papers on the table and leave. Mommy cries; she runs to the bedroom and collapses on the bed, still shrieking. Jenny's mom opens the door and peeks in; then she goes into Mommy's room and runs to her side. She holds her and Mommy cries into her shoulder. . . "

Frank shoots up from his chair. What is he reading? What's this his wife is writing? Is this the way her father was killed . . . Israel's Lebanon invasion back in '82? Oh my God, no wonder his death was traumatic for her. No wonder she's always been interested in this topic. He skims the next few paragraphs.

She tells me he'll never call again. I ask her if he's mad at me. She hugs me harder and says no. She tells me Daddy will always love me, but he can't call because he went to heaven.

I ask Mommy where heaven is. She says no one really knows, but good people go there when they die. My daddy was a real good person & a great dad; so that's where he is. I miss him. I will always miss him, and I will do my best to be a good person so I go there when I die and see Daddy again.

I want my daddy; I want him here with me, but he never will be. Mommy tells me he was killed when some bad people caused an explosion where Daddy was staying. Mommy says she will try to be the same person she was before Daddy died. But she never was. Neither was I.

Frank finishes the story and drops the paper. Instinctively he grabs his jacket, some notes, calls down the hall to his boss, "Production rates check. I have to leave. If you need me for anything, call."

He was hurrying home.

67

WADE REACTS

Wade had just concluded an all-morning meeting with executives and bankers. Outside funding for this project would be necessary for this development to be first class. Not only golf courses and club houses, but a full neighborhood of high-priced homes, pools, and tennis courts would be built for families who wanted more. He closed the deal.

"Lunch? On me," Scott offered. "It's a great project Wade. You did an outstanding job. Come on, let's celebrate. Our usual table, a nice lunch, cocktails?"

Wade shook his head. "Thanks, Scott, but I'll pass."

Scott gave a quizzical look. "You okay? You haven't seemed yourself for a few weeks."

"Nothing major. Have a lot on my mind."

"Well, if I can help, give a holler."

Wade nodded, watching the group head for lunch. He headed for his office.

"Coffee, Mr. Henderson?" His assistant knocked on his open door.

"Not coffee, but would you order me one of those hot pastrami sandwiches from Bernie's?"

She nodded and left. Wade took off his jacket and tie, opened the top button of his shirt, grabbed a bottle of tonic water, the paper and reclined in his ergonomically designed chair. If it went back any further, he would fall asleep.

He unfolded the paper and scanned. *So, she made the front page.* He seethed. *Wonder who she exploited to get this spot.*

When he got to her epilogue, he sat up straight, as Frank had. He read. His eyes swallowed every word. When he finished, he threw down the paper and put his head in his hands. *She never told me; she never told me, but did she have to?*

Of course not. It wasn't a badge she'd wear on her sleeve, maybe like something he had been doing for five years. When does the hurt go away? Maybe never, but she had gotten on with her life and done the best she could. For someone who had carried that nightmare around with her since childhood, she had done a pretty good job, much better than he had.

And no excuse that she had had more time. She was a kid. Her nightmare had been imprinted in her mind when she was four. She had decades of living without her father, not five years. Maybe his tragedy was worse if you wanted numbers and proximity, but losing her father to an attack was the same.

Would she accept his apology? Would she ever speak to him again? He didn't know, but he had to try. He called for Stan, grabbed his jacket, and hurried out as his assistant walked down the hallway. She held out his lunch as he passed. He waved her off. "You eat it, Karen, I've gotta run."

68

CASSIE REACTS

"Oh my God, Vaughn. Honey, have you read this? Have you read Stevie's story? My own daughter and I never realized how badly Brian's death had affected her. I knew it had then and for years after, but this much trauma and so long?" She shook her head. "It's my fault; it's all my fault. I should have been more aware. I should have been a better mother." Cassie began to cry.

"Hon, you were, and still are, a great mother." Vaughn sat beside his wife and put his arm around her. "You were dealing with the same tragedy, yet you doted on Stevie. Even before I knew how your husband had died, it was obvious Stevie was your first priority. "You were always there for her, shopping, baking for Christmas, sharing everything chocolate. It was always Stevie first. You could never have known she had retreated into this kind of a shell."

"I should have known; I should have asked her, opened up more about my own hurt which would have allowed her to open up about hers." She shook her head. "I alluded to it when Mason kissed her when they were here Easter, but I never pushed it. Then when she told me about Frank, I figured everything was fine and it was my imagining, but it wasn't fine." She looked up at her husband. "She must hate me."

"Hate you? Cassie, you're overreacting. Your daughter loves you. Come on, Hon, don't do this to yourself." He looked at the tears flowing down Cassie's cheeks. "Want to drive up?"

Cassie nodded. "Should we call first?"

"And take the chance of getting a no? Let's just go. I'll drive. No need to be chauffeured."

"I'll tell Julia. Maybe she'll want to come. She adores Stevie. As cavalier as she can sometimes be, I think she'll want to be with her sister. Vaughn, she must be so upset."

"She has Frank. He'll never let anything happen to her." He hugged his wife. "Same as I'd never let anything happen to you."

69

YEARS COME TOGETHER

F rank had expected to come home to an empty house, change into bermudas and a T-shirt, buy Stevie yellow roses then call her at work. If she couldn't talk there, maybe she could come home early and they could talk on the deck overlooking their water view. What he didn't expect, at 2:30, was his wife sitting on the porch chaise, rocking back and forth, sipping tea. She was facing the Hudson, and so engrossed in her thoughts she never heard him climb the steps.

"Hon," he whispered apprehensively, "Are you okay? Is everything okay?"

She turned. She had been crying.

"Let's talk," he said softly. She nodded. He sat next to her and took her hand. "I'm here, Babe. Always will be. We can overcome anything, together." She nodded. "What happened?"

"Jeff got fired, because of me; I got fired, because he knew his replacement would make my life hell." Stevie talked about everything in detail, how Jeffrey printed her story knowing he'd be terminated; that he fired her so she could get unemployment as she looked for another job, because she'd be unemployed anyway once his replacement set her in his sites; she told him about Jeff's new job and then she talked about her dad.

"He never came home. I never saw him again, not for birthdays, not for Christmases, not for summertime at the beach, and I never got over the trauma. I remember he used to spin me around so my feet would brush the surf. I couldn't have been more than three, yet I remember it as though it were yesterday. He'd laugh and hug me, and then he was gone, forever, because of an Israeli invasion.

"My mother didn't talk about it. She tried to go on as though nothing had changed, but everything had changed. I submerged myself in books, played with a few neighborhood friends who knew, but I never mingled with anyone else.

"In college, I made a few friends, not close enough to talk to them about my dad, but friendly enough to hang around with. Dating? You were right – I ran from men. Maybe if my dad hadn't been killed, I could have been secure enough to have had a relationship with a guy knowing I could get over it if he left, but I was too insecure for that. I subconsciously knew if the guy broke up with me, my dad being taken from me would resurface. I wasn't strong enough to relive that.

"Mason knew about my father. All the kids at Chelsea Academy knew, so it was different, safer. But anyone other than Mason, someone I'd have to tell . . ." she shook her head, "I wasn't strong enough to go through that either."

Frank put his arm around her and she nuzzled her head on his chest. "Life twists and turns us in ways we never expect. When it takes someone we love, especially at a young age when the memories we've made are few, there's a void. I wish I had known sooner so I could have helped you. I haven't been the perfect guy in your life. I hope you can forgive me for the insensitivities and hurt I've caused you."

She looked in his eyes. "You couldn't have known; I couldn't tell you, so what hurt is left for you to talk about?"

"At Ribs & Brew, when I left you to face that masher." Stevie's expression said she agreed, but she smiled remembering that. "And on your porch. That was crude, and I apologize. I know now, with what you've told me tonight and that night you showed me your dad's picture after Wade threw you out, you had never been with a man." Stevie looked away, chagrinned.

"I couldn't."

"Hey, I'm the one apologizing. I never imagined, ever, until we talked a little when you were clutching your dad's picture. How traumatic that must have been for you, having a boor like me do that. I will never forgive myself."

"Stevie smiled. "But it got us married, and that's a good thing."

"Yeah, Babe, that the best thing. You are the best part of my life."

They held onto each other for minutes that passed without either of them speaking. They watched clouds dance in a bright blue sky, and puffs of wind form them into clown faces, dragons, squirrels, and a cuddly raccoon. There was no need to talk. Right here, right now, all was right with the world.

70

OTHERS ARRIVE

The couple was inside pulling food out of the fridge to start some kind of dinner, nothing much, because Stevie could not eat. Her Lebanon story and its repercussions must have shocked her system; so Frank decided to cook something easy.

He pulled out a frying pan, a package of ground sirloin and was about to rip open the wrapper, while Stevie washed lettuce and veggies for a salad, when the doorbell rang. Frank gave a "Who could that be?" look, wiped his hands and went to answer. Stevie couldn't imagine who would be at their door. She liked her neighbors but they never dropped by. Then she heard voices, very familiar voices. *Mom?* She dried her hands to start for the door, but too late, they were already in the kitchen and her mom was walking towards her with open arms and a tear-strewn face.

"Honey, I'm so sorry. I should have done so much more to help you. I was buried too deep in my own grief to help you with yours." Cassie hugged her daughter. "Please forgive me."

Stevie fell into her arms and they both cried, cried for decades of sorrow over the loss of a husband and a father; cried for the cruelties of war and a government that forced us into them for its own agenda; and for the ephemeral nature of life. We're here today; we struggle with the good and the bad life throws our way . . . and then it's over. Life . . *a walking shadow, a poor player, that struts and frets his hour upon the stage and then is heard no more . . . a tale told by an idiot, full of sound and fury, signifying nothing.*

Frank and Vaughn both had tears in their eyes, Frank for the pain he never knew his wife had experienced, and Vaughn for a duration of cruelty after he knew how Cassie's husband had died. Their wives were beautiful and courageous people. Both men, in their own way, knew they had been blessed.

Not to be left out, Julia ran up to her mother and half-sister and hugged them. Arms opened up and brought her in; it was a circle of sorrow, but a stronger one of love and hope.

Then Vaughn announced, "Food." Boxes went onto the kitchen table and Vaughn and Frank began unpacking them. "Hope your grill works, Frank," Vaughn said as he opened butcher wrap, covering fillet mignon. More butcher wrap uncovered rib eye steaks and center cut pork chops. Loaves of artisan bread, containers of humus, cheese baked in crispy, flaky, phyllo dough, baklava filled with pistachio nuts and some filled with rich cream, Stevie's favorite since childhood, Greek olives, and so much more appeared.

"Where did you get all this?" Stevie marveled.

"We made a few stops." Cassie smiled.

"No one can eat all this," Stevie countered.

"But we can try," Frank said and clapped his hands together.

"Let's get started!" Vaughn announced.

The men went for the grill and the ladies transferred food to platters and bowls amidst Julia's non-stop talk. She talked about her upcoming trip to Ireland with two sorority sisters, her courses for the fall, boys she had met, some she liked, others she didn't and she talked about Samir and Travis and their summer jobs. That girl could talk about anything, and surprisingly, everyone listened. It was nice to hear the ebullience of youth. Stevie got in a few comments here and there, but she did not have her younger sister's gift of gab. Hopefully, the guy Julia married would be a good listener.

The dining room table set for five, the men brought in more meat than any of them could ever eat. "Any neighbors you want to invite?" Vaughn joked.

Unfortunately, no. Her neighbors were porch sitters, not visitors. Stevie had invited a few over for lunch way before she met Frank, but they had declined. Guess they thought the age gap was too wide. Too bad, because Stevie could converse with anyone regardless of age. She just couldn't talk as much as her sister.

Platters got passed around and plates overflowed. Stevie tried to eat, but she could not. Amidst comments about how good everything tasted, and how skilled the men were with the grill, the doorbell rang, again.

71

A VISITOR

S tevie and Frank looked at each other with a "Who could that be *now*," expression. "I'll get it," Frank said. "Don't wait for me."

A man's voice. Stevie had no idea who'd be stopping by at this hour. Everyone continued their dinner and conversation, listening to Julia chatter about changing her major, again, when suddenly, Frank reentered the room with Wade. All conversation ceased.

Stevie was stunned. Wade of all people. Wade, who had clenched his jaw, accused her of writing her 9-11 article to work her way up to a better job and had thrown her out of his apartment. That Wade, who never wanted to see her again, was standing in her dining room next to her husband, head down, looking in every direction except at her.

"Everyone, this is Wade Henderson, Stevie's . . . friend." Stevie gave him a look. That kind of look. "He's come to apologize to Stevie, so I thought I'd let him meet the family at the same time." Frank turned to Wade. "Go ahead Buddy, the audience is all yours."

Wade had come to apologize to Stevie, hoping she would see him, but he hadn't expected to apologize in front of her family. He glanced around sheepishly. *Say what's in my heart. May as well begin.*

"None of you know me, and I doubt Stevie wants to, for the hurt I've caused her, but I need to apologize and hope she accepts it.

"I met Stevie in Bradford County, where she was covering a story about fracking, where she met her husband, Frank," he nodded in Frank's direction. "He was the fracking commander for the project on my property. Frank's crew had just dug up a steel box that contained packs of United States Treasury bills, not Federal Reserve notes, and a hand-written note that asked, 'Who owns us?' Since it was found on my property, the strongbox became mine and the note became a quest.

"A quest, a four month quest Stevie and I undertook to learn the significance of these bills. Were we successful? Only in that I realized my great-grandfather was Louis T. McFadden, who railed against the Federal Reserve back in 1933, which led me to search for my relatives and find them, a very positive outcome. We also learned how closely linked our Federal Reserve is to European bankers and the Rothschilds, and how our country was duped into turning over monetary control to these vipers. Also that there is a tight connection to the Fed, Rothschilds and Israel which Stevie tied to 9-11.

"And that's where my apology comes in. You all know she wrote an outstanding story about 9-11, because she was there – dressed in a fireman's uniform to get the story first-hand. You also know she got her job from that story, but what Stevie didn't know when she was in that melee helping to pull out a young mother and her daughter, was that they were my wife and my daughter. They died on route to the hospital." Cassie, Vaughn, and Julia gasped. The room became eerily still. Wade passed his hand across his face, wiping away strands of tears.

"We continued our research until we realized Stevie's editor would never print what we had learned; there was no reason to go further. We had no proof. But what happened during our last meeting was that I realized Stevie was the reporter who had written that story, had written my wife's last words . . . and I became angry, very angry. I accused her of sensationalism to get a promotion, threw her out of my apartment, and committed myself to hating her for her lack of sensitivity.

"After I read her article about Israel's attack on Lebanon and read her epilogue, I realized my behavior had been outrageous. I had been acting like a jerk, and worse. I had to apologize for my behavior and for my hateful outburst during our last meeting. You didn't deserve that, Stevie, even if I hadn't learned about your father. I'm so sorry. Can you forgive me? Please?"

Quiet tears fell from her eyes. She relived flashes of her own pain she would never forget, but she would never let it dominate her life again.

Cassie cried from her own memories and the hurt her husband's death had caused, so many years; so many lives. She left her seat, came around the table and surprised Wade with an all-embracing hug. He didn't know what to do, pull away or hug her back. Stevie settled it for him by getting up and hugging them both.

"Of course I can forgive you, and I believe my mother can too."

Cassie nodded. "I can. I know what you went through, still are going through. No one can take their place, but someone can creep in alongside them. It'll happen. You'll see."

"Frank, you must have wanted to strangle me."

Frank nodded, "Close," then he smiled.

"Thank you, for having the courage to say how you felt." Cassie said. "Your wife and daughter would not have wanted you to live in the past, though, just as Brian would not have wanted me to. And look who God brought into our lives." She nodded towards Vaughn and to Julia, who seemed to blush. Wade pulled away, thanked them, and turned for the foyer.

"Where are you going?"

"I'll show myself out, Stevie."

"You will *not* show yourself out. Do you think we can eat even half the amount of food my mom and Vaughn brought, and Frank & Vaughn grilled? Oh, no. You have to stay and help."

If Wade had thought of protesting it would have been impossible. Frank dragged a chair to an open space at the table and indicated that Wade sit. Stevie brought a place setting in from the kitchen and Vaughn passed the meat platter his way before Wade settled into his seat. "Better hurry. This is heavy and it may drop." Wade took the platter, then sat. He was going nowhere.

And just like that, he had become part of their family. He ate heartily, enjoying every minute, every word of conversation. They all talked energetically, except for Julia who remained uncharacteristically silent. They

291

talked about future plans, travels, and work. They offered all kinds of possibilities for Stevie who'd be looking for a new job until Jeffrey called to tell her she'd have two pages of *Men's and Women's Health* magazine, if she wanted it, because she would have to accept an obvious cut in pay.

Yes, she wanted it, and could she divide her time and work from home? That was a yes. The family hooted and raised their glasses, even Julia got in on the toast, her first interaction since Frank had escorted Wade into the dining room. This time, for dessert, she got up to get Wade a dessert plate.

The evening lasted well into the night and Stevie's family, under duress of exhaustion, agreed to take the guest bedroom on the first floor. Julia would take the living room sofa. She didn't want to hear any sounds coming from the master bedroom.

"You little . . ." Stevie threw her napkin at her sister. "You watch your mouth." This time she was certain Wade blushed.

Close to midnight, Stevie and Frank walked Wade to the door, while the others finished second and third cups of coffee.

"Don't be a stranger," Stevie said.

"Come over and enjoy the view from our side of the Hudson," Frank added. "We grill a lot during the summer. We'd love to have you."

He and Wade shook hands; Stevie gave him a peck on his cheek.

As he started down the stairs, he paused "I was just wondering," he hesitated, "would you mind if . . ."

Stevie shook her head. "If what?"

"If I saw your sister?"

"'Saw'? Saw how, as in 'date'?"

Wade nodded, "Yes, as in a date."

"Julia? Wade she's nineteen, and you're . . . thirty-five. That's a sixteen year difference."

She looked at Wade, then at her husband, wondering why they were both staring at her. Then she got it. "Oh, no, oh, no, this is not the same. I'm not in college; I've worked close to eight years; I'm not a young ingenue, a sophomore who's already changed her major twice." She looked at Frank for support. "There's a big difference, right, Hon."

Frank looked at his wife who was trying to squirm her way out of this one. He shook his head. "Uh uh."

"It's different; it's different; it's different." She got no sympathy from either of them. "Okay, how about this: I'll see if there's interest on her part. If there is, and our mother approves, I'll give you the home phone number. But that's it. If she says no, there will be no further talk about the topic."

Frank and Wade smiled. "Fine with me," Wade said. "Thanks for the best evening I've had in years."

"Bye, Wade. You must visit again; it's mandatory. We'll call with an invitation if you prefer."

"If you don't, I'll call you with an invitation. Some very nice restaurants in the City."

They watched him get in his limo and head out towards the tunnel. "You think Julia will be amenable to a date with Wade?"

Frank burst into laughter. "You are brilliant in almost everything, Hon, but you are in denial on this one. Did you see the way she looked at him? Did you notice how your

293

garrulous sister clammed up after he walked through the door? She didn't utter more than five words all evening, except for her absolutely correct statement about sounds coming from the bedroom. How about we go upstairs and make some right now." He leaned her against the door sill and let his mouth caress her face."

"Frank, stop. Neighbors might see."

"Good, let them see."

He kissed her hairline. "You're going to be bored as hell working part time, and as much as I'd like to, I can't stay home and be in bed with you most of the day."

"I have a few things I'd like to do," she said coyly.

"Like what? Writing a book about something controversial?"

"Writing a book? That's a good idea, and in addition to my new part-time job, I might freelance for the local paper, and I need time to paint the spare bedroom, maybe pale yellow."

"Yellow?" He gave an ugh. "Why yellow?"

"Maybe pastel green, or pink, or blue, get some new curtains and a few mobiles and crib sheets, and . . . "

"By the time she got to 'mobiles,' he got it."

"Oh my God! Oh my God! Really? Your serious? You're pregnant? We're having a baby?!"

He hooted and hugged her tightly. He could not contain his joy, which brought the family to the door, wondering what the celebration was about. Two words from Stevie, "I'm pregnant," caused an uproar that could be heard down the block. They all hugged each other tightly.

Finally, they walked inside and closed the door on the past. A new life was beginning.

It could not have been a better day.

-THE END-

ACKNOWLEGEMENTS

A special thanks to my husband for proofreading and critiquing the manuscript, and to my immediate family who contributed their expertise in various sections of the novel. To my cousin, PhD, economics, thank you for critiquing several chapters, and a special thanks, also, to a gentleman in Bradford County, PA, who provided extensive information about hydraulic fracturing, fracking.

ABOUT the AUTHOR

Loretta J. Krause was born and raised in Paterson, NJ. She attended Montclair State University for both her B.A. and M.A. in English, and attended William Paterson University for full certification in mathematics. She taught high school English and middle school math

OTHER BOOKS by the AUTHOR

Barefoot to Palestine
(A novel set at a private academy in New Jersey, in 1987, four years after the attack on our U.S. Marine barracks in Lebanon)